UNWEPT

UNWEPT

BOOK ONE *of* THE NIGHTBIRDS

Tracy Hickman &
Laura Hickman

A TOM DOHERTY ASSOCIATES BOOK

NEW YORK

UNWEPT

Copyright © 2014 by Tracy Hickman and Laura Hickman

Designed by Mary A. Wirth

A Tor Book
Published by Tom Doherty Associates, LLC
175 Fifth Avenue
New York, NY 10010

www.tor-forge.com

Tor® is a registered trademark of Tom Doherty Associates, LLC.

The Library of Congress Cataloging-in-Publication Data
is available upon request.

ISBN 978-0-7653-3203-5 (hardcover)
ISBN 978-1-4299-5592-8 (e-book)

Tor books may be purchased for educational, business, or promotional use.
For information on bulk purchases, please contact Macmillan Corporate and
Premium Sales Department at 1-800-221-7945, extension 5442,
or write specialmarkets@macmillan.com.

First Edition: July 2014

Printed in the United States of America

0 9 8 7 6 5 4 3 2 1

To Carmen Agra Deedy and Laurie Johnson,
who listened to this story and heard the music in the words

CONTENTS

UNWEPT

1

NIGHTMARE

A cold, damp darkness greeted Ellis as her consciousness collected within her. She had been resting peacefully on her back. A sweet fluttering against her cheek brought her back from sleep. She raised a hand to touch her face and her wrist clacked against a solid surface inches in front of her.

Panic rose in her as the strangeness of being in a place she didn't recall brought her sharply awake in the midst of utter darkness.

She shifted and felt her shoulder blades slide along a slick hardness at her back. Her fingers ran along the surface too close overhead. It, too, was very smooth. The experience was an odd feeling—or, rather, non-feeling—for she couldn't perceive the weave of cloth or wood or of any subtle texture, only the hardness of the walls all about her. She jerked her elbows out in an effort to determine the width of the place she was in. They cracked dully against the sides of the light-less void in which she lay.

Darkness pressed down on her. A tightness in her chest made breathing impossible. Confusion filled her mind. She didn't know where she was or how she had gotten here. She moved awkwardly trying to fold her arms across her chest, as though to ward off the cold. Her arms clattered against her breastbone. She raised her head, her eyes trying to pry open the inky blackness. Nothing. She could see nothing. Terror gripped her as she shifted her head upward and her skull thumped loudly against the top of her tiny chamber. She lay back trying to quell the panic that made her mind race and her frame nearly immobile.

I can't be here, she thought. *Where am I? How do I get out?*

This last question became paramount. She wriggled about and found that she was so tightly enclosed that she could not even turn on her side. She stretched her stiffened legs out and stretched her arms above her measuring both ends of the damp darkness in which she lay. She slid her fingers about looking for a way out.

A latch, a knob, anything. She struggled and shook against the silkiness of her strange cocoon. She tried to cry out, but only a faint whistle of dry, brittle air escaped her stiff jaw. She raised her fists and began pounding on the slick surface above. Her fists made a strange clinking noise against the top of her confine. She jerked them back to her chest, where they clattered noisily. Bone met exposed bone.

Stone-hard fingers skittered up over her dry chest. Her bare ribs encased no beating heart, no lungs to fill with desperately wanted air. Her fingers skimmed upward, where they easily closed around the vertebrae of her brittle neck. She slid her skeletal hands up farther along her gaping jaw, where she could detect no flesh, no lips, only the constant and hideous smile of exposed teeth.

My skeleton.

Fear engulfed her as her boney digits explored the rim of the hole where her nose once was and finally found a resting place deep in her eye sockets. She arched her neck and opened her maw wide in scream after silent scream.

She lay back numbly. *My coffin. Dead . . . Buried . . .*

Bitter sorrow overwhelmed her terror and she tried to weep, but no moisture escaped the charcoal blackness of the empty eye sockets. She lay dazed and horror filled.

Is this death? Trapped forever in a box?

Silence rushed in, around and through Ellis. It was consuming in its totality. No breath rattled her chest; no breeze stirred; no bird sang. She lay in repose waiting to escape.

A sound, faint and almost inaudible, drifted down into her claustrophobic space. She became aware of the muffled cries of an infant in the distance far beyond the cold, damp earth above her.

A sudden, squealing sound of metal startled her. It scraped against the wood of her coffin directly overhead.

Help me! Please! She tried to call out, yet only managed to clatter her jaw awkwardly. She stopped moving and felt more than heard the rather rhythmic sound of scraping, followed by a dull thud, which caused her coffin to quake slightly. Someone or something was working directly above her.

They realize their mistake? They know I'm alive!

She began beating wildly against the lid of the coffin, ignoring the sound of her bones against the wood. She pounded forcefully and began to feel the lid give as she struck it. Air, fresh air, whispered through her restless resting place. Her need to breathe became sudden and immediate. The lid was giving way under her blows. She arched her spine and shoved.

Bones cracked and clattered. The clasp on the lid snapped under the force of her pushing. Air, mingled with the pungent smell of damp, fresh, mossy earth, rushed into her coffin as she slid one skeletal hand out around the edge of the lid.

"No!" A male voice rang out from above.

She sensed the weight of his boot as he stepped on the lid of her coffin and the clanging of a shovel against her bone-clad hand.

Help! Stop! I'm alive. Still no sound escaped between her teeth. She was desperate to cry out and knew it was impossible.

She jerked back her talon-like digits from the lid for fear of pain as they caught against the rim under the lid. She suddenly grasped that her bones were rock hard, indestructible. She felt nothing.

Bright anger mingled with the terror of being trapped again; she shoved mightily. Bones creaked; gaping jaw clenched; shoulder blades bit into the slippery satin lining.

The lid sprang open. Air! Ellis longed to breathe. She wheezed in determinedly between her whistling teeth.

I will breathe this air! she promised herself.

The dust rose up around her. Organs, muscles, sinew, cartilage, all gathered to her bones, forming around her writh-ing framework. Her beating heart pumped blood painfully through veins and arteries in a red liquid haze. And finally a soft downy covering of pink and cream skin covered all— cheeks, neck, breasts, stomach, back, hips, legs, feet and hands. Her hair caressed her form. She breathed in deeply, her lungs on fire with the rich oxygen around her. Ellis's body was awash in pain as her reunited parts regained life.

A groan, increasing to a full shriek, escaped her lips and her liquid eyes focused. She feebly pulled the flimsy coffin shroud around her weak and vulnerable form. More clearly now, she heard the soft cry of an infant in the distance.

A tall man stood directly above her exposed grave, a lantern in one hand and a shovel in the other. He held the lantern low by his side. He remained dark and faceless. Ellis was illuminated completely by the lantern and felt almost as though she could somehow slip into the light and away from here.

Questions raced through her head. But only a weak "thank you" escaped her parched lips. She lifted a frail arm, expectant of assistance from her rescuer.

"That body! It's an obscenity. How can I possibly help you now?" he said, biting off the words. He turned on his heel and threw down the shovel. The lamplight gleamed off the buckle of his tall, shiny boots. Ellis heard the digger speaking to someone in the blackness and heard an indistinct female voice in response. He retreated into the night, carrying the lantern and cruelly leaving Ellis again in the darkness.

"*Wait! I'm alive!*" she called out pleadingly. The figure did not or would not hear her. Ellis climbed from her coffin and out of the grave of fresh earth, which was moist, rich and oddly comforting, crumbling coolly under her aching hands.

She stood on a vast landscape of ruined buildings, scorched earth and desolation. The battleground stretched to the horizon under a leaden sky.

She stared back into the dark confines of her little coffin. Relief and revulsion swelled in her and she felt light-headed. She pulled the silken shroud about her newly re-formed, delicate body. Tears poured over her cheeks, her eyes rolled back in her head and a moan escaped her lips. The distant crying became more distinct and closer.

The dark figure wrapped cold fingers around her wrist and started leading her away. . . .

2

JOURNEY

Ellis! Wake up!

Ellis started and gasped awake. In the dizzy free fall out of sleep she gripped the arm of the cushioned bench. The train swayed and rumbled noisily beneath her. The Pullman car in which she rode was as much of a shock to her now as the dream had been. She took in the rich paneling of the walls, the gentle curve of the cream-colored ceiling, the maroon carpeting and the brass fittings in an instant. It was all very familiar and yet disquieting, as she could not remember boarding the train or, for that matter, the cushioned bench on which she sat.

She inspected her gloved hands. Their shape was familiar and unchanged by the ravages of her dream. She breathed in deeply, fully, and released it. The need for air was with her still. The last binding ribbons of sleep slipped away.

The only remnant of the nightmare was the persistent

crying of a baby. Ellis straightened up on her bench and looked about the small train compartment. A large basket with a squirming bundle rested on the facing bench across from her and was being studiously ignored by the thin, pinched-faced woman in a boater hat and nurse's uniform sitting next to it. The woman had set aside the paper she was reading and was now staring at Ellis with annoyance. The once-opulent rail-car was otherwise devoid of any occupants.

"Don't rouse yourself, dearie," the stick of a woman said, reaching across to pat Ellis's hands. Ellis recoiled a little at the stranger's gesture.

The nurse's eyes were as cold as the glass of her spectacles. "Poor thing, just be calm. Hush now; we'll be there soon."

Ellis felt confused, wondering why the nurse was saying to her what she should be saying to the infant. "I'm sorry, have we been introduced?"

The woman turned her bespectacled gaze on Ellis and spoke in flat tones. "In fact, we have and we've been through that already. I'm Nurse Finny Disir."

Ellis knew she should nod in recognition of the woman's introduction, but urgent, necessary questions filled her and spilled out into the compartment over the whimpering infant. "I'm sorry. . . . Where, where am I?" Spoken aloud, it was such a strange question that it fell thickly from her lips.

"Oh dear. I was concerned when you boarded the train that you were not quite yourself." Ellis doubted from the nurse's tone that the woman had been concerned at all. "Young lady, do you know your name?"

The baby's wails became insistent.

"I'm Ellis. Ellis . . ." Her voice trailed off as her tongue searched for a second name.

She could not recall. Ellis did not remember boarding the train or any details of their journey beyond awakening in the Pullman car. She strained to recall any little details about herself that one should easily know. She looked down at the green skirt she was wearing, its pleats falling to the floor over her high-topped kid boots.

I'm wearing these clothes, but this shade of green, would I choose it for traveling? She shifted a bit across the velvet cushion at her back. *Such a mundane, but odd, question,* she observed. The thought continued to spin in the air before her until once again her eyes fell to her gloved hands, which she greeted with familiar relief.

The dull green of her skirt gave rise to an inner certainty that she hadn't chosen it. "I don't remember this skirt. I feel certain I wouldn't choose it. It's ugly."

The nurse allowed herself a clipped smile. "Tosh, girl, what a thing to concern yourself with now. Your choice of travel clothing is unimportant. Please don't distress yourself over it. However, you were working through an introduction and having no name is of no use to anyone. What is your name, child? Of what family?"

Finny looked expectantly at Ellis, her eyes absurdly large behind her glasses.

The family name, I know it; I must. Ellis turned and sat blindly staring out of the window. A thick fog swirled past as the train rushed onward, affording only occasional glimpses of the trees, the brightness of their autumn colors muted by the dim light, rushing by. She focused on her reflection in the glass and studied her image, which to her relief was familiar. She saw a handsome young woman of about eighteen. Surely not so young as seventeen. Nineteen? Nineteen . . . Her hand flew to her hair beneath her bonnet. Short. *How long has it been like this?* She withdrew from this thought to concentrate on the question at hand, the rest of her name.

The name did not come, nor did a scrap of any other detail of her life. She struggled to remember anything before this moment. Panic rising in her throat, her tight corset lacings bit into her waist through her chemise, making it hard to breathe. Her interior architecture was all empty rooms and closed doors. She felt certain she should know—did know—but all that came were tears blurring the edge of her vision.

Ellis looked up with pleading eyes at the nurse. The nurse met her gaze over her glasses with what Ellis felt was more scrutiny than sympathy.

The baby's cries continued.

"The name you're looking for is Harkington. You've had a bad time of it. Don't strain; it will all come back."

Harkington. At least it seemed right. She'd been ill. They had cut her hair. She felt heartsick. Demands from an unknown life flooded Ellis. Past and present merged into question marks.

"Where are we going?" Eliis asked.

"You've been put in my care for a short journey to a place where you can recuperate."

"What hap . . . where . . . how?" As she found it impossible to form a single question with so many pressing against her mind, her voice trailed off.

"Land sakes, child," the nurse huffed in exasperation. "You cannot ask every question at once!"

A simple query formed that demanded an answer: "Where is my family? My mother . . . father?"

The baby wailed.

"All will be explained in time. They know where you are. You have been put in my care. I have strict orders from the doctor not to overtax you." The nurse sighed and offered a small comfort to the young woman. "I suppose it won't hurt to say we are going someplace you've been before—to your cousin Jenny's home, in Gamin, Maine. Why, she's just your age."

Jenny. This name called up a warm feeling of relief that wasn't quite a memory but felt as though it could become one.

"Jenny. Gamin. Yes, I think . . . well, I don't remember quite, but I will be happy to see her."

"Well, that's enough for now." The nurse snapped open her newspaper, closing off the conversation. The baby's pleas subsided into tiny hiccups and quiet breathing.

Ellis was surprised by Nurse Disir's abruptness. She found herself with a waking life that was almost as strange as the dream she had escaped. Finny, though dressed in the broad-brimmed hat and blue cape of a nurse, seemed anything but nurturing or helpful.

Glancing at the paper wall between her and her traveling

companion, Ellis furtively read headlines wondering if something from the everyday would bring back her memory. The tall words spouted the terrors of war in Europe. She took in a picture of people wearing gas masks and she tilted her head slightly to read the caption just as the nurse said, "If you truly wish to read it, Miss Harkington, I'll give it to you when we arrive later. Please just settle back and try to shut your eyes. I can't deliver you to Uncle Lucian in a state of nervous exhaustion."

"Uncle Lucian?"

"Yes, Dr. Lucian Carmichael."

My uncle is a doctor. I must remember. . . .

"Miss, get some rest, now." This was not a suggestion but a command.

Ellis leaned back and closed her eyes against the brightness of the compartment, the strangeness of her situation and the rocking of the train. She was exhausted and queasy.

Left to her thoughts, she found panic-driven tears welling up under her eyelids and her throat constricted tightly. She swallowed hard and tried to breathe. An unbidden and jumbled cascade of questions began to tumble in her head. She bridled them and began to sort her thoughts into some order.

What do I know? My name is Ellis. I am on a train. I have a cousin named Jenny. I have an uncle, a doctor. I am going to Gamin, a place I have been before. Traveling with me is Finny Disir, a nurse. I have been ill. Ellis shook her head at this; she did not know any of these things really, except that she was Ellis and she must have been, no, must still be ill. She sighed inwardly, exhausted by the enormity of the small questions she could not answer. They flooded over her and swirled away any sense of reality. *Where is home? Who do I belong to? Where is my mother? What happened to me? Am I going to be well? When will I remember? Remember . . . Remember . . .*

The crying began again, and seeing that the nurse was totally absorbed in her paper, Ellis stood in the gently rocking train and stepped around her to look at their third traveling companion. Blue ribbons fringed the basket. A boy. The baby's fists beat wildly at the air. A small patchwork quilt of blue and yellow lay in disarray around his tiny form. Ellis reached forward to touch his palm. His tiny hand closed about her finger. Ellis made cooing noises to soothe the infant and reached her free arm around the baby and swept him from the basket. The crying stopped. Relief and silence filled Ellis as she cradled the child. The baby looked wide-eyed at her and she wiped his wet cheeks. Ellis smiled and sang softly:

> *"Over there, over there*
> *Send the word, send the word over there*
> *That the Yanks are coming . . ."*

"Stop that!"

"Stop what?"

"Put that down this instant! You shouldn't be holding an infant."

Ellis froze in place with the child, a feeling of defensiveness stole over her and she straightened and came to her full height in the train compartment.

"I don't feel weak. Besides, he's more content being held."
She smiled down at the baby, who smiled back. Peace settled in
her chest for the first time since she'd awakened. She plucked
and smoothed the quilt around his form and made certain her
grasp was firm but gentle. "He's fine. What are you doing
here, little fella?"

The train shifted and lurched across the tracks, causing Ellis
to almost lose her footing. She staggered and swayed with her
bundle, dropping back safely into her seat.

Finny stood, folding her paper abruptly, bending toward
Ellis and the baby. "Young woman, until you are turned over
to Dr. Carmichael, you must do as I say. You've been placed
in my care and for now I know what is best."

She scooped the child from Ellis's arms and with a deft
motion deposited him lightly back in his basket. He chuffed
in protest, inhaled deeply and let out a protesting wail in response.

"But I'm sitting now. Please just let me—"

"No."

"Please."

"No, it wouldn't be safe for either of you."

Ellis could not fathom the implications of Finny's words.
Either of us? It made no sense.

"Nurse Disir, isn't he in your care, too? Shouldn't you be
holding him?" Ellis felt sympathy for the infant with his renewed cries and her indignation overthrew politeness. Ellis's
frayed nerves were jangling. Her "nurse" didn't seem to understand what either of her charges needed.

"Really, it's not to be borne . . . my patients telling me

what to do," Finny muttered, and grappled with her now-rumpled newspaper. She readjusted her boater hat firmly on her head, and as she squared her high-necked cape on her shoulders she met and locked with Ellis's level, sober gray gaze.

"Nurse, I may have to mention to the doctor how distressed I was about the baby's weeping." The continued gaze lasted until the nurse broke it off, looking into her lap.

"Fine. Please don't mention the baby to the doctor." Finny shook her head ruefully. "You were never one to be trifled with, miss. "

She felt the pleasure of winning a victory for her tiny companion. Then Ellis inhaled an "Oh" of surprise as she suddenly understood from Finny's comment that she and the nurse had known each other for some time.

"Oh, stop looking like a fish; we are old acquaintances! Don't think they'd trust you to just anybody? Here, if I'm not going to finish the paper then you might amuse yourself with it for a while." She shoved the newspaper into Ellis's gloved hands and leaned over the baby boy, clumsily caressing and clucking him into a tearstained silence. Ellis opened the newspaper and stole glimpses over the paper's edge, thinking how very peculiar the whole scene was.

"Please don't stare at my back, young woman; I wouldn't want to report your odd behavior to the doctor, either."

Ellis shivered in the heat of the train compartment, wondering at the uncanny perceptiveness of the nurse. She leaned into the faded red velvet cushion of her seat wishing she could disappear into it. She allowed her eyes to drop down the page of headlines.

War. War in Europe. *Yes,* she thought. *I know that. France and England fending off Germany. Our soldier boys are over there. But the fighting isn't here, not yet.* News of the everyday world was both comforting and disquieting.

She read about the picture of the people in gas masks. It was from Boston. High-society matrons modeled them to raise awareness of the need for donations of walnut shells and peach pits to make charcoal for the masks' filters.

She turned the page and found a long article detailing two recent murders in a string of murders in Halifax. Ellis glanced furtively above the top edge of the page to be certain the nurse was still busily engaged with the child. She glanced down again at the article and knew that this was what had kept the nurse's rapt attention against the crying of the baby. Ellis also knew that it was inappropriate reading for a young woman such as herself. She dove into forbidden territory.

The illustration accompanying the article showed the body of a woman lying in an alley, her face obscured by a military coat. Two policemen were lifting up the coat to examine the face of the victim and both were in apparent shock at the visage. The headline read:

IMPASSIONED PREDATOR
THIRD MAIDEN MURDERED IN NEW BRUNSWICK
Citizens in Grip of Fear

Ellis read down the lurid column through the sketchy details of the death of a young woman. The killer was unknown, but it was thought that this case related to others. Wondering just how close she and her companions were on the map to these murders, Ellis shivered, and the vague feeling that she had known the victim slipped into her thoughts. *It's impossible.*

The squeal of the coach brakes filled the air. Ellis's head snapped up, jolted away from the story as the train perceptibly slowed. Outside the window she could see the hats of people on a train platform sliding into view. The fog outside appeared to be retreating, though the pall still remained.

"Finally!" Nurse Disir stood adjusting her clothing and scooping up the basket. "Your baggage claim check is in the right pocket of your jacket, miss. I'll take my leave of you here, as I have a pressing errand."

The nurse hoisted the basket elbow height in emphasis and turned on her heel to leave just as the train came to a stop.

"Wait! Aren't you going to introduce me to the doctor? How will I know him?" Ellis half-stood trying to get her footing on the still-lurching Pullman to follow the nurse.

"Don't be a silly goose. He's Uncle Lucian; he'll know you." Finny's words were tossed over her shoulder as she disappeared out of the train door.

The abandonment of her nurse shocked Ellis into uncertain silence. She glanced about the empty train compartment and filled with trepidation she stepped quickly through the door into the vestibule. She moved at once down the coach's stairs and onto the station platform.

The nurse had already vanished into the crowd.

3

END OF THE LINE

Ellis stood on the platform next to the train, smoke and hot steam sighing loudly about her. The morning fog receded, slowly revealing a large crowd of people milling about, greeting one another beneath the roof that sheltered the long platform. The throng wound in and around one another with greetings and laughter. There was a cluster of soldiers near the far end of the platform on the other side of the station house. They soberly stood apart from the main crowd who blindly moved around them. It seemed no one had come to greet the soldiers and the rest of the people were determined not to acknowledge them.

Ellis was certain she knew none of these people and was disquieted when she became aware that a number of people were furtively glancing at her. Among them was a young girl with large violet eyes clutching sheet music and a dark-haired artist with her easel, paint case and canvasses in hand. Many in the crowd openly ogled Ellis. She tried to avoid their gaze as she tried to see if she could somehow divine which among them might be the doctor, her uncle.

She fingered the baggage ticket in her pocket, wondering if someone here had a similar ticket with which they might claim her. Her lips moved as she went over the short litany of things she had been told about herself.

I am Ellis Harkington; I have been ill. I have been sent to Gamin to get well. My cousin is Jenny. My uncle is a doctor who should be—

"Ellis, at last."

—here.

Ellis looked up into sharp green eyes placed in a craggy face shaded by a straw skimmer set at a jaunty angle. He had a square jaw and a clean-shaven face wrinkled and weathered with age. His ears looked too large for his head and, though largely hidden beneath his hat, his white hair stuck out at wild angles.

"Dr. Carmichael?" She deflated a bit as she took him in and realized that she felt no recognition.

"Uncle Lucian to you, my dear." His face split into a gap-toothed grin. "It took me a moment to spot you in the crowd. Where is your nurse?"

"I don't know. She left the train in a great hurry with a baby. She . . . she . . ." Ellis wondered how to explain the nurse's odd actions.

"Never mind that now, dear girl. I will speak with her later. Baby, eh? Well, they can be an awful lot of trouble." His voice was gentle, but the green eyes looked stern. "So, missy, how many pieces of luggage will I need to load into the Steamer?"

Dr. Carmichael ushered her through the platform's doors into the large, enclosed waiting room inside the station house. Ellis could smell the freshness of the paint on the gingerbread-trimmed beams supporting the roof above them. Ceiling fans with tinkling crystal teardrops circled slowly overhead, scattering small rainbows about the walls and stirring the damp air above the crowded room. Polished brass shone brightly on all the fixtures. It was opulent for such a small town. The beveled glass doors were open on all sides despite the crisp autumn air.

"Over here." He guided her by the elbow to a corner near the ticket desk where a single large trunk sat alone. He bent to hoist the unwieldy piece. Ellis jumped as it slipped and thudded to the floor.

"Let's be certain it's mine." Ellis offered him the baggage claim ticket. Once again she felt the eyes of the crowd following her, and she felt her cheeks grow warm.

"It's the only piece here, girl." He looked about for a porter and then bent to struggle with it again and gazed at her from his awkward angle under the trunk. "I'm sorry, Ellis; I should have known you wouldn't recognize it. It's just that we have so few travelers stopping here, it just couldn't belong to anyone else."

Ellis nodded politely wondering what he was talking about. *Few travelers?* The station had been jammed with people when she arrived. She stole a glance at the now-thinning crowd, many of whom were now openly staring at her.

"Ellis." It was a deep, husky sound murmuring her name behind her. She turned to see a man stepping out of the crowd. He was handsome—too handsome, Ellis thought, in the way that some women wear too much perfume. He was clean shaven, but there were the shades of a dark beard remaining about his strong jaw and cheeks. His hair was carefully groomed but long in a way that was no longer fashionable. His manner suggested that he did not care about fashion. His eyes were a striking light blue, intense and somehow sad, like a dog that had been beaten and did not comprehend why.

"Don't mind them; they are all agog about any outsiders," he said with an ingratiating smile. He was certainly older than Ellis. He wore a morning coat, waistcoat, striped pants and, incongruously, bowler hat.

He strode up with a young woman on his arm. She had luxurious blond hair beneath her wide-brimmed hat. She was about Ellis's age and gazing at her with a look that left Ellis uncertain. At the man's words the crowd began to dissipate.

"Merrick. How good of you to come." The doctor allowed the heavy trunk to slide to the floor once more. Ellis wondered exactly what she saw in the old man's eyes as he spoke to the younger man. Fear? Respect? The look was gone like the shadow of a cloud moving across the sun.

"I wouldn't have missed this for anything." Merrick sighed through a beaming smile that made Ellis blush.

"Merrick, would you be so good as to take this woman's baggage to my auto?" Dr. Carmichael gestured to the large trunk beside him. "It appears to be too heavy for this old man."

"Not until we've said hello." In a breach of decorum he snatched up her hand before it was offered. The smile he beamed down on Ellis was at once charming and sad. Ellis gauged him to be a number of years more mature than herself, perhaps almost thirty, but could not determine his age. She took in the look in his piercing blue eyes, which both terrified and thrilled her at once. *How ridiculous I am*, she thought, mustering common sense and brushing off the fleeting tingle up her spine.

"Oh! I believe we have met," she stated simply, feeling she finally understood the situation.

"Why, yes! Do you know me?" Merrick pressed in close to her, too close, retaining a firm hold on her fingers. Ellis retreated a half step. He gazed down on her so earnestly that she wished she could tell him yes, if only to escape his intense scrutiny.

Lucian stepped in toward them. "Merrick, I believe it's quite obvious that the young lady is being polite. She doesn't even know her own baggage yet. Allow me to reintroduce you: Miss Ellis Harkington, this is Mr. Merrick Bacchus, benefactor of the entire town."

Merrick tipped his hat graciously and let go of Ellis's now-numb fingers. "Glad you've safely arrived, Miss Harkington. May I see you safely to Summersend?"

Ellis surprised by the offer, wondering what he could mean, looked up at her uncle.

"Now, Merrick, we've talked about this. I will take Ellis to her cousin Jenny's. If you would just be so good as to get that trunk in the back of my car."

"She'll freeze in that rattletrap of yours, old man. At least my auto is enclosed. Besides, Alicia wants to visit with her."

Ellis glanced at the woman still clinging to Merrick's arm.

Alicia was still staring back at her in such a way that Ellis was not all that sure that "visiting" was what the woman had in mind.

Dr. Carmichael shook his head. "There will be plenty of time for visits and parties and all those things you young folks like—"

Merrick interrupted, turning toward Ellis. "Let's ask our guest what she wants."

The young lady who had been grasping Merrick's arm through the whole proceeding quietly cleared her throat and stepped forward, closing the tight circle. "Do let us take you out to Summersend, my dear Ellis. Merrick's motorcar would be far more comfortable for you, and besides, we haven't seen you for so very long."

Dr. Carmichael gestured to the young woman. "This is Alicia, Ellie. She is a very old friend of yours."

Both the young ladies nodded politely.

Ellis could see the couple was keen for her company, and it was heartening to be so welcome in a strange place, even though this pair's country manners were overbearing. "Thank you for your kind offer. I think for now I should stay with my doctor and go straightway to see my cousin Jenny."

"That is exactly what I am offering you, Miss Harkington. Summersend is the name of Jenny's cottage." Merrick continued to press Ellis to go with him.

The lobby of the train station was warm in the confined space and was made all the more uncomfortable by the press of strangers. Every time she took a step back, Merrick pressed forward. Ellis felt the heavy layers of her green traveling suit become warm and prickly. The spinning fans above afforded no relief. Light-headed, Ellis swayed.

Merrick dropped Alicia's arm to catch Ellis. He wrapped an arm about her waist in support, which was both a relief and shocking at once.

"We've kept you standing here too long," he whispered. "Let me help you to the car."

Before she could protest, her uncle came to her rescue. "I'll help my patient, young man. You get that trunk." He turned to her. "I'm so sorry. I'm a fool for keeping you standing here. I'm sure you're exhausted. Can you walk? My motorcar is just outside."

Dr. Carmichael helped her out through the lobby doors and down the station steps. The fog had thinned considerably now and Ellis could see the shapes of the town buildings down the road through the fog. Merrick followed them out with Alicia. He did not have Ellis's baggage but had, rather, two young men he had selected from the crowd haul the trunk behind them.

The Steamer sat just at the base of the stairs. The yellow spokes and rims of the tires were clean, supporting the chassis and brown body on leaf carriage springs. The vehicle was charming—"quaint" came to Ellis's mind—but its steam boiler hissed ominously. The doctor helped her into the car. She felt revived by the gentle fall breeze and sunlight as she sat on the passenger side of the automobile.

At Merrick's direction, the young men placed the trunk into the backseat. Merrick then leaned over the car door and whispered to the doctor, "I'll let the constable know she's here and safe. He'll be relieved."

Ellis's ears burned at his words and her jaw tensed. *Whatever did he mean by that?*

Alicia came trailing behind him, carefully skirting the soldiers on the platform and looking downcast. Ellis could not catch her eye to smile in parting.

The doctor tucked a blanket across Ellis's lap, then swathed her in a driving veil and goggles. The doctor situated his own hat and goggles and engaged the steam. With a chuffing sound that slowly increased in tempo, the Steamer began to roll and they set out for Summersend cottage.

And Jenny, Ellis reminded herself.

The glory of autumn foliage·blazed red, orange and gold in the breaking afternoon sunlight. The fog had given way to a brilliant blue sky that contained cotton ball clouds. She mused that the scene looked like a child's idyllic painting as they rumbled along. She reflected on how exhausting and confusing the day had been.

She spied under her lashes on her uncle driving the car. She opened her mouth to speak, but he just shook his head, smiling kindly.

"I can see you are all question marks over there. You wouldn't want a moth to fly into that pretty mouth. Best wait."

She was left to consider her strange new existence in silence. *People know me, but I don't know them. I've been sent far from home to recuperate. Why? The whole town seemed aware of my arrival. Do they also know about my illness? What do they know about me that I don't know myself? Are Merrick and Alicia truly old friends of mine? Why did the constable need to know I arrived? Will I remember Jenny?*

The thought of Jenny was the one Ellis focused on as the rhythmic rumble of the car engine became soothing. She slid down and tilted her head back on the seat, rearranging the blanket to cover her arms and chest, and allowed her shoulders to slump beneath it. All but her tight lips and jaw, which held a press of unspoken questions, relaxed. She breathed in the chill autumn air as she passed below the shadow of tall, ancient trees displaying their fall finery. The passing scene took on a blurred glow through the netting of the driving veil.

Behind her the train gave a warning blast as it chugged out of the station. It wasn't until they arrived at Summersend that Ellis realized she hadn't seen anyone from the large crowd step up from the platform and board the train.

4

JENNY

Jennifer March, called Jenny by her friends, walked with purpose down the road leading along the low crest of Pearson's Point from town toward her home. She bore two heavy baskets of groceries that she shifted from side to side in the crook of her arm, trying to avoid her touching her gloves as she did so. Merrick had promised to meet her in town and give her a ride with her burden, but at the appointed time he had not arrived. She'd set off on foot, hoping more than believing he would show up. She should have taken the horse cart from home but found it difficult to hitch it up, let alone wield the reins. So instead she had had to walk all the way down the road that ran from Gamin in a long crescent around the bay to her home on Pearson's Point. It was a pleasant journey for the most part as she walked in the scent of the windblown pines and the autumn hardwoods that lined both sides of the road. Yet now her arms were aching and her hands were bothering her again.

She looked with displeasure at her gloved hands, their deformity hidden under soft gray kid. *The accident.* She frowned at the ground and took a longer stride, her petticoats swishing in a large arc as she quickened her pace.

If I weren't weighed down with this food nonsense I could be standing on the shore down from the house by now. But she continued to hold her burdens because she knew she must, and here on the solitary road her thoughts kept pace with her.

It was strange to think about what had happened the last time she'd seen Ellis and that Ellis had no knowledge of it. Jenny had been warned that Ellis most likely would not remember anything, not even her. *How can she not know me?*

Jenny sighed, patting the cloth of her gloves and giving them a tug to smooth them out. She gave herself over to the memories Dr. Carmichael had helped her piece together in the days that came after the game. That late-summer day she and Ellis had been playing on a path between the woods and a fenced pasture that confined a herd of cows. *Was it fair or cloudy?* Jenny shook her head, not remembering, but every other detail was painfully bright.

"I know a good game! Let's find the old gate that leads to the Garden of Wonders," Ellis said. Ellis plunged off the path and into the woods.

"Ellie, no!" Jenny trailed reluctantly behind her.

The Garden of Wonders was an old and childish game they played, which usually devolved into hide-and-seek. The gate was never found, of course, but remained compellingly elusive and just out of reach.

"Merrick doesn't like these woods. He won't like that we are playing here."

"He's not king," Ellis tossed over her shoulder. "Besides, some of our friends are supposed to be out here, too."

Jenny made a sour expression at Ellis's back but tried to match her steps to Ellis's as her cousin chanted the old riddle that marked the start of the game:

"The old gate is high and heavy and hidden
Till you choose to be chosen it is forbidden
The toll for passage is the age of a man
You cannot go back the way you began.
What am I?"

Ellis sprinted forward deeper into the bramble-like woods. "I can hear our friends, Jen; we've just got to catch up."

Jenny didn't hear anything but her own ragged breathing and the occasional scurrying of a surprised squirrel whose kingdom had been trespassed upon. "Please, Ellie, let's go back to the house. We can get some lemonade and look for seashells on the point," Jenny begged.

The thorny bushes became thicker and snagged Jenny's skirts and scraped her arms, but Ellis went ahead heedless of Jenny's words. Jenny lagged behind without enthusiasm. She'd lost sight of Ellis but could hear her crashing through the thick woods. Jenny looked up in surprise as she heard several squeals of delight just ahead.

"There it is!" said a young male voice. "Shove harder! Push!" A cheer of several familiar voices rose up just beyond her in the thick underbrush.

Jenny tumbled into a small clearing where she saw a tall door-like *gate made of broad oak planks set into a stone wall. Her eyes grew wide as she ran forward just in time to see Ellis pushing hard against it and peering through the slit of the opening. It couldn't be real. It couldn't, thought Jenny.*

"Don't go, Ellie. You don't know what's over there."

"Come on, Jenny; this is our chance to see the Garden of Wonders. Don't you want a little peek at least? The others are already in there. It's getting harder to hold it open. Help me!" Ellis leaned her face forward into the opening.

"Ellie, it could be anything in there. You don't know where it goes. Come on; let's go back."

"But the others have already gone in!" Ellis protested.

Jenny, whose words were having no effect, yanked on Ellis's hair.

"Stop that!" Ellis reached back, keeping her shoulder jammed against the gate, and shoved Jenny roughly. Jenny grabbed Ellis's hands and the girls tugged fiercely at each other. Ellis slid around to face Jenny and dug her heels into the soft earth beneath her while shoving her back against the gate to keep it ajar. Neither girl was willing to relinquish her hold upon the other.

Suddenly the dirt gave way beneath Ellis's feet and as she lost her balance all her weight fell against the gate. Ellis stumbled backward, letting go of Jenny's hands. Unwisely, Jenny grabbed the other girl hard by the wrists. Momentum pulled them forward but not fast enough to save Jenny from what happened next. Ellis tripping backward through the opening, ripped free from Jenny's grasp. Ellis fell completely through the opening. The gate swung back quickly with a sickening thud, hitting Jenny in the head, crushing and dragging her hands along the stonework to where the gate and the wall met as one. The last thing she

heard was the clanging of the gate's latch into place. Hands crushed
and captive, head bleeding, she fainted against the now-closed gate.

That was the last time she had seen Ellis. This was the
memory that she'd pieced together with the help of Alicia and
others.

Jenny had been plagued with headaches and a spotty
memory in the long days that followed. Her hands were thickly
splinted and bandaged. She'd been placed in the care of the
Disir sisters, who fed her soup and kept up a constant prattle as
they quibbled and gossiped across their quilting frame, threaded
needles in hand.

Jenny eventually thought to ask them about Ellis, who had
not come to see her since her accident. Clucking their tongues
over the pity of her plight, they told her that Ellis was no longer in Gamin but had been taken to the city. Jenny felt ill
inside that her dearest friend had not come to comfort her.

The time came when the doctor removed the gauze and
splints. Jenny's hands were weak, deformed things; her fingers would not straighten out properly. Uncle Lucian gave
her a hard rubber ball to squeeze to strengthen her hands and
gave her a packet of willow bark tea in case she felt pain. She
had never used either of them.

Life had changed, of course. The piano at Summersend sat
silent. *I only ever tinkered on it a bit anyway,* she acknowledged.
She'd had to find ways to adapt to working with her now-
inept hands or ask others for help. Most folks in town had
been helpful for a while, but they wearied of it, though they
would never say so. Merrick had been the most persistent in

his assistance. She had felt so frightened and awkward in social situations. She had wondered if people would treat her differently now because of her strange hands and found it easiest to avoid gatherings. As she thought of how Merrick had saved her from shutting herself away she warmed and was grateful to him for including her in the literary social club, many parties and events in Gamin. He was her hero. *Except for today,* she thought tartly, but smiled anyway.

Jenny looked up, realizing she had stopped walking at some point in her reverie in the middle of the lane and had just stood staring into the past. It was time to move on. The gravel crunched beneath her boots as she stepped forward.

She didn't blame her cousin for what happened, an accident to be sure, but she wished Ellis hadn't gone away so fast. Now Ellis had come back, in trouble herself. Jenny understood the pain of not being able to recall the facts about one's life, though through the kindness of the doctor and friends she had come to know most of it and indeed remembered a good portion of it herself. Where Ellis was concerned, though, Jenny's memories seemed to be striddles and riddles, as the Disir sisters would say. Merrick and the doctor had encouraged Jenny to spin the rags into stories to comfort Ellis. It seemed that for now pretense and pretend would be the kindest memories of all. In time it would all come back, Merrick and the doctor had assured Jenny. The one story that was brightest in her memory was the one she was determined never to speak aloud again to Ellis or anyone else. The gate story would remain untold.

Jenny had been asked to help Ellis convalesce. It was the

opinion of the doctor that the quiet offered by the seclusion of Summersend was just what was needed and that Jenny's company just might be the tonic to heal Ellis's woes. He told Jenny he hoped she and Ellis would help each other.

Jenny rounded the last turn in the lane as the gables of Summersend came into view. Gamin Harbor lay sparkling beyond the house and grounds dancing in the sunlight, free of shadow. Her heart lifted at the sight of it. *I won't be "poor Jenny." It's not who I am today,* she mused. She shifted her burdens again and walked onward knowing that she could hike up her skirts and wade barefoot into the brisk waters of her little cove unseen by anyone except the gulls. *What shall I be today? A stranded mermaid?* A smile edged its way up her lips and she took a deep breath and plunged forward as though she were at the water's edge already.

5

SUMMERSEND

The sprawling architecture of Summersend welcomed Ellis and her pulse quickened as Dr. Carmichael's automobile chugged around a bend in the lane and brought Summersend into view.

The tenseness in her jaw relaxed.

There was the tiniest chiming in her head of something that was not quite a memory but familiar here and helped her breathe easier. The Victorian home was three stories tall if you included the cupola with its widow's walk, a vision of round turrets, conical roofs and bay windows. She felt she might know where the rooms in the house were placed, as though she could draw a map of the interior. Her gaze took in the clean lines of its many windows and high gables that were held in the embrace of a wide wraparound porch, which disappeared behind the house. Red climbing roses mingled with clematis winding about the heavy porch columns. The entire garden was blooming like summer in the autumn sunshine. Ellis breathed in the air. The mingling floral scents to her mind smelled of lilacs, though of course it was too late in the season for the purple blooms. She smiled and turned her face up to the light as the sun warmed her shoulders. She stood in the picture-perfect sun-drenched garden as her eyes swept up to take in the roofline set against the impossibly blue sky. She longed to stand in the cupola and look out on the sea.

Safe haven. Somehow my home.

Before the Steamer had completely stopped, Ellis jumped out of the vehicle and climbed the wide, clean steps up onto the porch.

"It's so wonderful, Dr. Carmichael!" she exclaimed.

"Yes, I suppose it is." The doctor set the brake on the car and awkwardly climbed down to the ground. "I would've thought Jenny would be out here waiting for you."

The doctor stepped up to the door and twisted the knob on the doorbell. He frowned down anxiously at his pocket watch. When there was no immediate answer he tried the latch and found the door unlocked. With a glance at Ellis and a shrug, he stepped into the cool darkness beyond and called out, "Jenny! Jenny! Your guest is here!"

Ellis hesitated to follow the doctor across the threshold, it seeming rather odd to walk into a house where the occupants weren't at home.

"Come in, girl," the doctor beckoned. "Jenny won't mind. You're expected. I just can't imagine where she's got to."

Ellis moved tentatively through the doorway and up a step into a small foyer. This, in turn, led to an archway and to a

short hall with double doors on either side and the main staircase rotunda beyond.

Dr. Carmichael stood in the hall, his slider hat in his hands.
"I'm sorry, but I'll have to leave you here; I have someone to
see."

"You have an appointment with another patient?" Ellis
asked, trying to understand why the doctor was leaving her
so abruptly.

"Just so, m'dear."

"And you'll be back this evening?"

"Well, no, not today." The doctor fidgeted. "But I will
send word to Jenny when it's time for your examination."

"Uncle Lucian, I don't understand. Aren't you . . ." She
weakly gestured about the room with her gloved hand.

"Ah, I see what you're wondering, girl. You thought I was
Jenny's father." He wheezed out a soft laugh, gave a half-
embarrassed grin as Ellis's face fell in unpleasant surprise. "No,
I have no children. Never married. Everyone just calls me
uncle here, out of respect for my age. Not really anyone's uncle,
I guess."

"Nurse Finny said you were my uncle." Ellis's voice had
an accusatory edge that trailed off into uncertainty. "She
tricked me." A sinking feeling washed over Ellis. She had
been wrong about one of the facts she thought she knew. It
was a blow; she knew so few things about her world.

"She did, did she?" He rocked back on his heels thoughtfully. "Well, I expect it seemed easier at the time. I apologize.
I must have a talk with the nurse about a number of things."

"Well, where do you live then?" Ellis asked.

Dr. Carmichael looked as though he were about to speak but then cocked his head to one side and showed a thin smile. "What's the grandest home you've ever been to see?"

Ellis blinked. "Well, I don't . . . I don't recall. . . ."

The doctor's face broke into a strange grin and he cleared his throat. "It's called the Norembega. It's Merrick's home and he allows me lodging there. It is a big rattletrap for two bachelors, so he lets me keep my offices there as well."

"If I've seen it before," Ellis said, "perhaps it will help me with my memory."

"But you did see it," Carmichael said quietly. "We passed it on the road on the way here. It's just at the top of Pearson's Point."

"But I don't recall—"

"You're tired." The doctor bowed slightly. "I'll take my leave, then."

"Wait, Doctor! Are my real aunt and uncle, I mean Jenny's parents, at home?" asked Ellis, wondering whom she could truly claim as her relations in this small town.

"No, child. Jenny has been on her own for some time."

Is Jenny older? How long has she been here without family? Is she truly living alone in this large house? Are we to have no chaperone? Ellis inhaled to begin a line of inquiry about her absent relations and the general situation, but the doctor was already heading out the door.

Ellis followed him to the door. "Please, Doctor, I've so many questions—"

"Now, don't you go traipsing about town till I have a chance to examine you thoroughly and don't let Jenny wear you out. I must come to understand your condition and exactly what we are dealing with." Seeing Ellis's forlorn face, he continued, "I expect you are a bit tired; get some rest. Sit in the parlor till Jenny shows up. And don't worry; I know you are no danger to yourself or anyone else. Besides, this is Gamin. Nothing ever happens here."

He chucked her lightly under the chin, then trotted down the porch steps. Glancing back at her, he tilted his hat at a rakish angle while touching its brim. "Good day, dear Ellis. It's good to have you back and with any luck you will be right as rain and your old self in no time."

He hopped into his car whistling a jaunty tune. It was obvious to Ellis that he was relieved to drop his obligations to her as he sped away.

"Not my uncle," she breathed out as she watched him go.

Ellis shut the front door and took a step into the entryway. She stood there for a moment in puzzlement, then suddenly realized something vital.

My trunk!

She whisked the front door open to call after the doctor, but there was nothing but a haze of dust hanging in the air where the automobile's wheels had churned the gravel and smoke from the Steamer's engine. She closed the door once again. *Well, he'll be back. I don't even know what's in the trunk anyway,* she thought wryly. *Anything would be better than this dusty green traveling suit. . . .*

Ellis froze as she stepped from the entryway farther into the house.

Her trunk sat squarely at the base of a broad circular staircase in the rotunda, just past the entryway.

When did he do that? Ellis thought. The sinking feeling
she'd had minutes earlier intensified and she became light-
headed. She couldn't seem to get any air into her lungs. She
found a seat on the front-hall bench next to an enormous and
ornate grandfather clock. The hands were motionless and the
clock did not tick.

Across from her, on a side table, sat an enormous bell jar
on an ornate base of darkly stained and lacquered wood. Inside was a piece of wood and pinned to that a single large luna
moth.

"I know just how you feel," Ellis muttered, tapping the
dome of glass.

She leaned her head against the clock case and shut her eyes.
*Am I still ill? They said I was getting well. He must have brought
the trunk in; I just don't recall it. Is this my life now? To see and not see,
to know and not know, to remember my name, but little else? Should
I tell someone about the trunk? Who? The nurse who plays tricks or
the doctor who is not my uncle?*

She swallowed, determined that Jenny would not find her
looking so helpless. Breathing evenly, though the weight of
what had just happened pressed down on her, she lifted her
head and looked about the entry. She glanced down the wide
hall, which spilled into a narrow interior rotunda that held
the sweeping circular staircase that wound its way up to the
second-floor landing. She allowed her eyes to ignore her trunk
and continued to examine the room. At the base of the stairs

the parquet floor was inset in the pattern of a map's compass. The compass points were inlaid with gold, as was the vining pattern that circled it. Across the rotunda was a set of doors. On her right and left more doors. *Which way to the parlor?*

Ellis rose and walked across the entryway and stood on the compass of wood and gold on the circular floor at the base of the stairs. Nearing the trunk for which she felt an odd distrust, she unbuttoned her traveling jacket and, removing it, nonchalantly placed it across the upended trunk along with her gloves, as though to put the unruly luggage in its place. She stepped onto the compass and, extending her right arm outward and covering her eyes with her left hand, she smiled and spun around on the compass. Just as her head felt a pleasant dizziness she stopped abruptly and opened her eyes. Her arm was pointing to the double doors back down the hall that were just to the right of the front door. She crossed back to it and opened both doors to peer inside.

It was a charming irregularly shaped room. The oddity was caused by the wall just to her right that rounded with the rotunda on the other side of it. She saw at once that although there were various comfortable chairs and the occasional end table scattered about the room, this was not the parlor but the music room. A red mahogany butterfly baby grand piano sat in the sunlight that shone through the windows. She could see from the doorway that though the piano was finished with a high polish it was dusty. She crossed the threshold to the piano, forgetting about the parlor.

She sat down on the bench and pressed her fingers lightly against the cover and pushed up. The polished wood folded back along the piano hinge. The keys gleamed under the light from the window next to it. Ellis pressed the tips of her fingers lightly against the keys' cool surface, her hands in a careful and practiced arch. The instrument responded with a run of notes and a pair of exquisite chords sounding in response to her hands. Ellis smiled for a moment, but then her hands hesitated, faltered and stopped. She realized she could no longer remember the piece. It was frustrating, for the music was in her but unremembered. She struggled a few more times but at last dropped her hands in her lap in disgust. *There must be something here I can play.*

She stood and brushed her hands together and then along her skirt to remove the dust. She opened the bench looking for sheet music. But it was empty and there was none on the piano itself. Her lips tightened in disappointment. She spied a bookcase in the far corner of the room where the circular wall met the wall opposite the doors. She crossed the room, curious to see if it held sheet music. It held knickknacks, seashells, dead flowers in a vase and the covers to a few songs, but no actual music.

How odd.

Ellis, feeling some temerity, picked up the vase, thinking she would ferry the dead flowers to the trash for her cousin. As Ellis reached for the vase she stumbled, her hands catching the edge of the bookcase. She heard a tiny click, the bookcase swiveled slightly toward her and she felt a puff of air. She gently tugged the case toward her and found that it was not only a bookcase but also a door that swung open from another room.

She took the vase in hand and she stepped in, thrilling to the prospect of a secret room. The wall to her right was lined with cupboards. On the wall opposite the door was a long row of windows set high into the wall. Bright light spilled into the room from above. In the center of the room was a little treadle sewing machine, a chair and a long rectangular table covered with dust, like the piano. A workroom, she thought glumly. She wondered about the contents of the cupboards. *Linens? Cloth for dresses?* She stepped through the door and set the vase on the table. As she opened the first cupboard, which was empty, she heard a gentle click behind her. She spun around to find only a blank wall where the door had been moments before.

That's not possible.

Not seeing any other exits, she sprang to the wall where the door had been. She pushed against the wall in the place she judged the door to be, but it seemed to be solid wall and would not give way. *A door in, but none out? I shouldn't be poking around in someone else's house.* What seemed like a bit of innocent snooping just moments before now felt like a serious mistake.

She slid her hands over the wall and finally found a hair-line crack down the wall where the door must be. Scrabbling her fingers along the door, she looked for a latch. She stepped back from the door and leaned against the table edge. She picked up the cutting shears next to the sewing machine with the thought of prying open the door somehow. She tried to push the sharp tips into the crack, but the gap was much too narrow. She dug into the wallpaper and hard plaster around the crack but succeeded only in marring the wallpaper as the shears slipped skittering along its surface. She set the scissors on the table in disgust, knowing that after making such a mark on the wall she wouldn't be able to keep her misadventure a secret.

Earlier, standing in the sun outside, she thought she knew the layout of the house. But this place was not familiar. The feeling of being trapped suddenly overwhelmed her, drawing up memories of her earlier nightmare. She suddenly began yelling, banging her fists against the wall.

"Hello, can you hear me? Jenny, I'm in here!" she yelled over and over again at the invisible door. She knew her cousin had most likely not yet returned. In a few minutes Ellis's voice grew hoarse and she leaned heavily against the wall. She was ashamed and afraid. She'd been impulsive in deciding to explore the house on her own.

She took in deep breaths, chiding herself to remain calm and allow reason to prevail. *Could there be another way out?*

Swallowing hard, she smoothed her skirt and hair and looked around the room to consider her options. The high windows were too far out of reach even if she stood on the little chair next to the sewing machine. *As a last resort, I will find a way to break the windows. Perhaps someone will hear glass crashing even if they can't hear me yelling in here.*

Wondering how soon it would be wise to carry out her more desperate plan, she walked about the room inspecting it. *If there was another entrance into this room where would it be? Under the windows to the outside?* She slid her hands along the length of the wall, walking counterclockwise beneath the windows looking for another hairline crack in the wall. *No. Who brings mending in from the garden anyway?* She determined to circle the room and continued to slide her hands across the corner of the room and onto the wall directly to her left, across the room from the cupboard she'd opened. It was smooth under her hands and she had to brush away the memory of her nightmare on the train. The wall ended in a narrow wall set at a forty-five-degree angle attached to the wall she had entered through. Instead of a rectangle, the room was an odd lopsided pentagon.

She stood back to look at the angled wall. There was a small watercolor of a shipwreck on a rocky shore hanging on it, painted in bright colors in childlike strokes. As she spread her hands to either side of the wall her fingers detected on her left that which she had been hoping for: another hairline crack. With all her might she pushed against the wall. It swung open easily and she fell headlong in a heap at the base of the double doors just beyond the rotunda. She found herself staring back across the parquet compass toward the front door, the grandfather clock and her trunk. She shakily stood up, looking back at the portal to the sewing room: another bookcase. This bookcase had a vase similar to the one she'd moved earlier. She tilted her head to one side and, reaching out, lifted the vase. After a few seconds it swung shut, clicking into place. She replaced the vase.

She smiled sheepishly with relief. *What a strange mechanism,* she thought. *It's not safe, really. I'll have to mention it to my cousin . . . as soon as I feel comfortable enough to confess my folly.*

Ellis peered cautiously through the large double doors and found an enormous but welcoming room beyond. *A salon for entertaining, surely not the parlor.* Before her were wide windows overlooking the gardens, and to her left windows overlooked a broad lawn, which disappeared down a gentle slope toward the sea. A large fireplace was the focal point in the far corner of the room. About the fireplace were nestled divans, overstuffed chairs and little tables, each with a scattering of little knickknacks. Ellis might take pleasure in examining them later, but now her eyes were on the garden. Her greatest desire was to find a way outside and perhaps just rest on the porch till her cousin arrived. A door stood open at the far end of the salon and Ellis entered it, finding it to be a formal dining room. Immediately to her right were French doors leading out on to the back porch. Without hesitating, she opened the doors and walked out of the house into the autumn air. The back-porch steps led her down to a flawless bower of pink roses welcoming her. Beyond that was a shallow grassy hill that led downward toward the water's edge.

A gentle ocean breeze drifted up the low hill. Ellis found it a pleasure to walk over the perfectly manicured expanse of thick green lawn. Just below the clipped grassy hill was a white picket fence with a small gate in the middle.

Ellis shaded her eyes from the afternoon sun and looked at the small beach and sparkling water just beyond the gate.

There at the water's edge was a young woman with her white muslin skirts tucked up into the wide blue brocade belt at her waist, legs exposed. She was twirling at the water's edge chasing the tidewater that sprayed up onto her legs.

Jenny. She knew it was Jenny. Ellis's heart beat faster.

"Jenny! Jenny!" Ellis waved and ran down the hill toward

the little fence. The young woman looked up and gestured in return, running up the hill toward the gate and Ellis.

"Cousin Ellis!" Jenny clasped Ellis awkwardly across the gate. Ellis returned the embrace and sighed. She didn't recognize the young woman's face as she'd hoped, but somehow in touching Jenny she felt happy.

Ellis opened the gate. Jenny rushed through, her words tumbling out before her.

"Did you just get here? Is the doctor with you? Did you bring lots of party dresses? Do you like lobster? I should have been at the door to greet you. We have so many things planned for you! Is your trunk upstairs? Did you meet anyone from town on the way in? How was your train ride? Would you like to see your room? There are so many handsome young men in town just now for the fall house parties. You'll have to meet Merrick; he's by far the handsomest. He's my beau, you know. Is that shade of green popular in the city? It reminds me of a soldier's uniform." Jenny pointed at Ellis's skirt.

Ellis had opened her mouth several times in an effort to answer Jenny's barrage of questions, which quite took her breath away. Finally perceiving a moment's hesitation, she looked up, smiling, and simply said, "No, I don't think so. In fact, I can't stand it." The girls' eyes met in merriment. Their laughter spilled out and floated out across the water.

"I can see you're travel weary. Here," said Jenny, taking Ellis's hand in her scarred right hand. Jenny tucked Ellis's hand into the crook of her elbow. As she did so waves of relief poured over Ellis. In this moment she felt safe. Arm in arm they strolled up the lawn toward the house.

"Your garden is lovely; it still looks like summer," said Ellis.

"Oh, do you really like it? I was hoping you would. Merrick thought you would like it, too. He helped me with it. You always liked summer best. Did I mention he's my beau?"

Ellis wondered if the very important-seeming Mr. Bacchus had actually been trimming the hedges in the garden. It seemed unlikely.

Ellis hesitated, not knowing how to respond. She knew it must show in her face, for Jenny chortled lightly and said, "Forgive my blithering. I'm just so happy to see you. I know I probably shouldn't ask, but do you remember anything yet? Do you remember me?" Jenny looked into Ellis's eyes with such hope that Ellis wished she were good at lying so she could tell her yes.

"Well, I'd have to say that beyond knowing my name, I don't know anything much. I have a million questions I'm just bursting to ask you."

They sat down on a porch swing and gazed out over the water.

"Where to begin? Please tell me something about myself, my family, where I'm from, anything at all really," begged Ellis.

"Oh, dear Ellis, I wish I could!"

"What do you mean?"

"I once lost memories, too, and the doctor and Merrick helped me piece my life back together again. This is one of the reasons you're here, because they believe I'd understand better than most how you're feeling. I wish I could tell you things, but the doctor would be unhappy with me. He says your case is different than mine and it is very important for you come to remember on your own."

Ellis struggled with tears. Two spilled over the rim and down her left cheek. This was not the answer she was hoping for or one she understood. She now knew why the doctor had dodged answering any questions in the car.

"Tears. I wish I could put them in a bottle, dear Ellis. It's going to be fine somehow; I promise," and Jenny leaned forward, touching more than wiping them away. "I recall less about you because of my accident than some of the others, I guess. I'm sure you will begin to remember soon."

"I wish I had some proof that I'd been here before . . . that I know this place . . . that I belong. I wish I just had a picture, a photograph, of the two of us." Ellis tilted her head down and away from Jenny's awkward ministrations.

"I think it's quite possible, now that you mention it, there is a picture somewhere in the house. It's very important to you, isn't it?" Jenny twisted the muslin of her skirts in her fingers, looking thoughtful.

"It would make all the difference to have something tangible."

"Tangible," Jenny echoed the word, and her eyes brightened. "Well, if we found a picture, then you'd just be looking at it, right? I mean, I wouldn't have *said* anything. I couldn't be accused of breaking the rules."

Rules? Jenny thought. *What rules?*

Smiling at each other, they jumped up from the porch swing and arm in arm strolled into the house.

6

DISTANT THUNDER

The sound of a low rumble rolling over the ocean woke Ellis. The morning air beyond the snug warmth of her quilt was chill. She struggled to hold on to sleep as a thin slice of morning sunlight slipped through the drapes of the French doors and fell across her face. She opened her eyes and they focused on the tiny framed photograph on the bed stand next to her.

Jenny had brought it to her last night. It was a picture of two young women. One of the women had long, flaxen hair and bowed lips. Alicia, Ellis supposed, as Jenny had said so. The image certainly looked like the woman Ellis had met hanging on the arm of Merrick the day before. The photo was grainy, however, making it hard to discern whether the features of the second young lady were Ellis's own. It was obvious that the porch in the background was Summersend. From hairstyles and apparent ages it looked as though the picture may not have been taken too long ago. She ran her fingers across the glass, studying her face and form in the picture. It seemed to be her and somehow more herself than she presently felt.

She dropped her hand away. *It's because I knew myself then.* She breathed in envy for the certainty that she had known in the moment the picture was taken. Ellis was now keenly aware of the gift in conviction of one's own identity. It was silly, she knew, but she would have been more comforted if the photograph had been of her with Jenny and not Alicia. She knew she should feel lucky that Jenny had bent the doctor's rules a bit for her sake. It was harmless enough to have the picture and no real help except that she now knew she'd been here before. And that was much more than she could claim yesterday.

Sliding her feet from beneath the covers, she reluctantly placed them on the dusty wool carpet beneath her feet. When she first entered the room last night, she was struck by the beauty of the vaulted ceiling. A pair of French doors led to a tiny, private balcony with a view of the bay and a narrow stair up to the widow's walk. The ornate wood-carved canopied bed commanded the room. The down quilt on it was embroidered with soft pink roses like those in the garden below. The scene called to Ellis's heart. Someone knew what she would like . . . perhaps even more than she did.

The room was lovely but on closer inspection not really ready for a guest. The bedding was the only thing in the room that wasn't covered in dust.

Her eyes lit on her trunk, next to a large armoire.

Ellis frowned. *How did it get up here?*

Ellis had wanted to ask Jenny about the trunk last night but thought better of it. If Jenny saw Ellis's dismay she kept it to herself and no explanation was forthcoming about the dusty room or the trunk. These things were just another oddity on a long list in a very odd day. Ellis had shrugged her aching shoulders into the nightgown Jenny produced for her use. In bed she had closed her eyes tightly, pushing away thoughts of the train and the nightmare as a deep weariness stole over her. Jenny had made her feel welcome. The smooth keys of the piano had felt good beneath her fingers, though she was unable to play a tune. Sleep wrapped her in a sweet, dreamless oblivion until the sun found her.

But the trunk was in her room all the same when she awoke.

Ellis dressed quickly in the heavy green skirt and cream blouse from the day before. She glanced at the trunk, which she hadn't touched last night despite Jenny's urging, and wished that when it was opened she would find something prettier and more fashionable than what she was wearing. But there was something about the trunk's peculiar movements she didn't trust. The smell of breakfast wafted into her room and she followed her nose downstairs to the dining room.

The large dining table was set for two at one end and several chafing dishes crowded the place settings. There was a newspaper neatly folded next to one of the plates. A small envelope casually lay to one side of the folded paper. She picked up the envelope and was surprised to find it addressed to both her and Jenny. The flap of the envelope was simply tucked in the back. Ellis gingerly opened it and found an invitation to a luncheon given by Alicia for later today. She let out a breath she'd been holding, disappointed that it was a mundane luncheon invitation. She had to smile wryly. What had she been expecting in the little note? A grand missive explaining all the missing pieces to her life? She knew it was rude to read the mail without Jenny, but any little bit of information she could gather was welcome. She carefully slipped the note back into the envelope and replaced it on the table.

She wondered where her cousin could be and peeked around the kitchen door to see if she was still in there cooking. Jenny was not in the kitchen, nor were there any dirty pans or other signs that a meal had been prepared there.

"Do you need something in the kitchen?" Startled, Ellis jumped back from the door and ran into Jenny, who was directly behind her.

"Oh, so sorry! I was looking for you, actually. The kitchen is so clean. How do you do it?" Ellis blurted out.

Jenny led Ellis back to the table, smiling. "I don't. I mean I don't cook, not really. Ever since . . ." She held up her maimed right hand. "Folks from town are always dropping things by. One of the Disirs must've brought this. I recognize the chafing dishes."

Ellis smiled stiffly and wondered about such casual country manners that neighbors didn't even knock or make their presence known. "Is that how my trunk got upstairs to my room? A neighbor?" They sat down at the table.

"Well, yes, at least I think so. Merrick promised he'd help me, but he was late. He must have toted it upstairs while we

were down in the garden. I wish he'd stayed to visit. . . ."
Jenny's voice trailed off as she removed the lid from the first
chafing dish, revealing eggs and sausage.

Ellis uncovered the second dish and helped herself to but-
tered toast. She glanced down at the newspaper by her plate
and realized that the little invitation that had been lying next
to it was now missing. She looked about the table and glanced
on the floor by her feet but saw no sign of it. Jenny looked up
questioningly, but Ellis busied herself with the paper, all curiosity about the missing envelope disappearing as she read the
headline:

SUSPECT SOUGHT IN GRISLY MURDERS
Down East Region Uneasy in Wake of Killings

There was a halftone photograph of a young woman accompanying the article. The original image must have been
slightly blurred, as the woman's features were indistinct. The
shape of her eyes, however, reminded Ellis strongly of the girl
with the striking violet eyes she had briefly seen on the railroad station platform just the day before. She moved on from
the grainy picture and began reading the text of the article
beneath.

FROM OUR CORRESPONDENT IN GAMIN: The citizens of the
entire coastal region rest uneasily this morning after police
reported the fourth in a series of violent and horrific slayings
of young artists. The latest foul deed was perpetrated two
nights ago in the vicinity of the docks in the port city of Bar

Harbor. Presumed dead is Philida Epstein, a pianist, from Portsmouth, New Hampshire, who suffered partial dismemberment. The police initially had difficulty identifying the victim of this heinous crime in part due to the extent of disfigurement inflicted on the woman's features. Notably, her hands have not yet been recovered.

The police continue to investigate although, as with the other cases, leads remain few. The coroner reports the woman initially died of blood loss and internal trauma due to numerous stab wounds to her body and the slashing cuts about her face. Presumably the more horrific aspects of the crime occurred after her death.

The three other victims: Miss Amanda Delacourte, a dancer from Bangor, Maine, discovered garroted and disfigured in Halifax, Nova Scotia; Miss Julia Carter, a poet originally from Salem, Mass., found bludgeoned and stabbed in Moncton, New Brunswick; and Miss Hepseba Lindt, a seamstress from Gloucester, Mass., garroted and maimed in St. John, New Brunswick, in a manner similar to Miss Delacourte.

Merrick Bacchus, leader of our community, was quick to comment on the events: "Our lads are across the seas, battling in this war to end all wars and facing the cruel privations of that conflict . . . now we good citizens of Gamin and our neighboring environs are threatened with those very horrors visited upon our fellow citizens. We must be vigilant against the outsider—the foreigner who is visiting such evil among us." Merrick called upon Police Captain Michael

O'Meara to bring all the force of the constabulary to bring this renegade to justice.

Captain O'Meara has been in consultation with officers to the north who have been following this string of deaths on our Down East shores. Some of those intimately acquainted with the investigation have alluded to a special witness—currently sequestered—who may have been the survivor of a previous attack in Halifax and from whom authorities hope to gain the identity of the monster-at-large.

Citizens are urged to lock their doors, travel in the company of friends and remain at home at night.

The toast was bland and cold in Ellis's hand. Ellis shuddered and put the paper down and tapped it. "Did you put this here?"

Jenny looked up. "Oh no. I don't really care for papers much. One of the Disir sisters must've brought it with breakfast, I'd guess. They have a penchant for the sensational." Jenny asked, her eyes round, "Do you think it's true?"

"I don't like to speculate about such things."

"It says they 'sequestered' someone," Jenny continued. "What does 'sequestered' mean?"

"It means they are hiding a witness who may have been attacked before." All the questions that Ellis had put aside to find sleep last night circled hungrily around her. A chill slid down her spine. *Am I the "sequestered witness"?* She desperately needed to know about herself and the people who seemed to be caring for her in this place. Was Jenny really her cousin or just a watchdog? Both? Did she need to escape this place or to hide here in the shadows? Had something horrendous happened to her that was too horrible to recall? Ellis looked across the table at Jenny. She suddenly needed to know what had happened to Alicia's invitation. She put down her fork and stood from the table. "Look, I know the doctor doesn't want anyone to tell me about me. But perhaps you could give me a tour and tell me about yourself and Gamin."

Jenny's eyes brightened. "I can do that without breaking the rules, I'm sure. But the doctor said—"

"I need to see to a few things upstairs this morning. Please consider it, Jenny?" Ellis said, thinking of how she would sneak out if Jenny refused.

"You wouldn't unpack your trunk without me?" Jenny smiled.

"Oh, of course you can help me unpack, if you wish. I just need to tidy things up a bit." Ellis watched as Jenny patted the pocket in her dress and knew where the envelope was.

Jenny seemed to sense what Ellis was saying. "Oh, the room wasn't quite right, was it? I am sorry. I should have given it more thought. I must learn to do these things for myself. I'll come tidy up your room, I promise, but first, let's go look at your dresses! I'm just bursting to see what you brought."

"Then we can talk while we unpack," Ellis said, wondering how she would get that envelope out of Jenny's pocket.

The girls opened the enormous wardrobe trunk and its contents spilled out like treasure across the carpet in Ellis's room.

"Look at this shoe!" Jenny scooped up a low-heeled bronze satin pump that had a buckle set with amber glass stones.

Ellis's hands caressed the fine silk, georgette, crepe and jersey gowns piled high within the trunk. Lacy camisoles, stockings and other underthings were neatly tied up in a brown paper parcel, as though they had never been worn before. Everything she could need for a prolonged stay had been provided. Ellis wondered for a moment whether she had packed the trunk herself. More likely someone else had packed it for her, and her brow furrowed at not knowing who that might be.

As she unpacked and handed each piece to Jenny she felt disappointment in not recalling owning such lovely things. "I know this seems strange, but I really don't feel like these are mine."

"Well, this is your trunk, isn't it? I wish it was mine. So many pretty things, city things." Jenny held up a deep blue silk drop-waist frock. "I think the city styles are wonderful. The skirts are slim and they are shorter. The turn of your ankle will definitely show when you're wearing this."

"I like the things in the trunk; they just don't seem like mine." Ellis sighed. "I know it doesn't really make sense, but somehow this is a deeper knowing than not remembering my life. I feel like I'll remember everything in time, but these clothes seem . . . foreign."

Jenny, who was trying on pairs of gloves and shoes as quickly as she could change them, answered, "Foreign? What country are they from?"

Ellis smiled as she shook her head slightly. This was not helping her get closer to the truth about herself.

"Let's just put this away and we can sort through it later to see which shoes go with which handbag and hat." Ellis picked up the parcel of underthings and a magazine slid out from beneath it. Jenny snatched it up.

"Fashions! Oh, look, Ellis, so many pictures of clothing. They remind me of your dresses. Skirts are so slim today and a bit shorter. I must seem so out-of-date to you. And look, so many of the young ladies have short hair like yours!"

Ellis grabbed the magazine and flipped through the pages. It was true, not only did her clothing seem to be very much like those pictured here, but also her hair was cropped short with bouncy curls at the nape of her neck like most of the women posing in the illustrations. She let out a short laugh. "I was sad because I thought my hair had been cut short because of my illness. Now I find out I'm a fashion plate." The girls' eyes met over the top of the magazine and they giggled.

"I'm chic!" Ellis said, exaggerating a demure model's pose. A thought lit Ellis's eyes. "Well, if we aren't going to put this all away in an orderly fashion right now, I think the only thing to be done is to put on some of my new rags and go into town."

Jenny paused a moment and replied, "The doctor said not to go traipsing about until he'd examined you."

Ellis watched Jenny's reaction and knew if she pushed her just a little she'd give in. She'd given Jenny a good reason to produce Alicia's invitation. Ellis was desperate to explore and to try to find her forgotten life. "The doctor is an old lemon! Come on; we're about the same size; you could pick out one of my new dresses to wear. Let's go have some fun."

"You really are feeling better this morning." Jenny began fingering the blue silk dress. Ellis smiled knowing she'd won as Jenny continued, "You really must see Gamin again. Just think, you might remember something! And besides, I want to take you to the Nightbirds House. Here." She withdrew the invitation from her pocket and waved it in the air. "Alicia has invited us into town to lunch. I just didn't want to say anything if you weren't up to it."

"What is the Nightbirds House?" Ellis asked, waves of relief pouring over her at the sight of the small piece of paper. *Perhaps I am just an invalid and not a prisoner after all.*

"It's where the local young people go. The full name is the Nightbirds Literary Society House. Don't worry; no one will actually make you read anything if you don't want to." Jenny smiled.

"What do they do there?"

"We plan outings and play games. We encourage each other in our creative pursuits. We each have—" Jenny stopped speaking and just looked at Ellis, waiting.

"What? Have what?" asked Ellis.

"Just come and see, please?" Jenny pleaded.

Ellis wondered how much of Jenny's desire was to show her the town and how much was to show off Ellis's new frocks. It didn't matter.

Ellis had tilted her head to one side while listening and allowed Jenny's words to appear to persuade her. "Why shouldn't I have a little outing . . . especially if it brings to mind anything about my life?"

"Yes. Let's go. We'll both pick something out to wear. I

want to wear the blue jumper with the embroidered medallions!"

Ellis sighed inwardly. It was the one she would have selected. She smiled her agreement and picked out a rust-colored mid-calf-length silk with a deep *V* in front that was inset by a lacy cream chemisette and had a sailor collar of chocolate brown velvet that ended in tassels at each corner. The close-fitting underskirt matched the collar. It was topped off with a poke bonnet that contained a spray of satin roses.

In the end, as the girls fussed with each other's buttons and hair, it was discovered that the blue frock was meant to be worn with an elegantly embroidered and crocheted Castle Cap that Ellis said looked like a sophisticated "Dutch girl's" hat. It became rapidly apparent that the cap would not fit over Jenny's hair piled high on her head. Laughing, Jenny surrendered the blue dress and gladly wore the rust-colored one Ellis had chosen.

Ellis checked her reflection in the glass of the stilled grandfather clock as they went out the door. She saw a smiling girl, ready to meet a new world.

She wondered who that girl was in the reflection.

7

GAMIN

The town of Gamin could be seen just across the waters of the bay from the back porch of Summersend. From that vantage point and from that place Gamin looked to be less than a mile away to the southwest. However, the road wound its way north and west back up the spine of Pearson Point for nearly a mile before it came to High Street. Only then could Ellis and Jenny turn southward again toward town. This more than doubled the distance to Gamin, but the morning sun warmed Ellis's back as she and Jenny walked together along the road banked with autumn colors. Ellis enjoyed the easy amiability of Jenny's sometimes peculiar chatter.

"You'll love our literary society." The gait of Jenny's step struck Ellis as somewhat pained, although Jenny herself did not seem to notice it. "We were so lucky that it didn't burn down."

"Burn down?" Ellis asked.

"Oh yes." Jenny had the peculiar habit of revealing the most alarming information at the strangest of times. "The fire happened about a week ago . . . or was it two? It was quite devastating to many of the buildings in town, although gratefully not our literary-society building or any of the really fashionable shops. Dr. Carmichael thinks it was an oil lamp that started it. It's not on Main Street, you know, but just off Main. Quite exciting, really . . . the most exciting thing to happen around here until you came. The church burned down completely."

"How dreadful!" Ellis said intently. "Was anyone hurt in the fire?"

"Not that anyone knows of." Jenny shrugged, then with a secretive smile leaned closer to Ellis as they walked. "Although I *did* hear someone was *missing*."

Ellis felt a little faint. "Then someone *was* lost in the fire?"

"No. No, I'm sure they'll turn up eventually." Ellis waved her crippled hand dismissively. "People always do, don't they? I mean look, *you're* here, aren't you?"

"I don't follow you, Jenny."

"Call me Jen. It's what you used to call me."

"And what did you call me?"

"Ellie, sometimes."

"Now, what does my being here have to do with people turning up?"

"It just seems like forever since I've seen you is all, and here you are."

"So who is it that has been missing since the fire? Where have they been?"

Jenny glanced at Ellis from under her eyelashes, and even before she formed a response Ellis somehow knew it would not be a whole answer. "He couldn't have been in the fire. I mean he had no reason to be in a building on Main Street, really."

"Who?"

"He's just one of us . . . one of the Nightbirds."

"That's such an odd name." Ellis sighed. "I wonder if I'll ever get used to it."

"Our literary society?" Jenny laughed. "Back when you were here before you used to—oh, sorry. It's all rather scandalous, actually. Sometimes we break rules and challenge society and are a bit mischievous. Still, being in the burning buildings would not have been part of the game that night, so I'm sure Ely wasn't there."

"Is he just out of town, perhaps?"

"I don't know, really. I'm just sure he'll be back, though." Jenny abruptly changed the conversation. "I'm getting it cut, you know."

Ellis looked at Jenny's face. She looked a bit anxious. Ellis supposed that Jenny felt somehow she was breaking the doctor's rules by discussing the missing person. Maybe it was someone Ellis had known quite well.

"What's his name?" Ellis was not quite ready to release the previous subject.

"It's Ely—Elias," Jenny said. She bit her lip before continuing, "It'd be best not mention this to the others."

Ellis smiled. She instinctively knew that the boundaries between her and Jenny were far softer than Jenny was willing to admit.

Ellis found that she liked the young woman strolling next to her and for Jenny's sake silenced, for now, all the questions on a continually growing list of things she didn't know about herself. She was treading blindly through a thick intellectual fog, stumbling over the pebbles of things that felt right, but without true recall. If she could find one familiar thing, perhaps it would all come back and she'd be able to enjoy this little visit and then go home.

". . . Should I?"

Ellis brushed aside her thoughts and looked up. Jenny was yanking on a tendril of hair that had escaped from beneath her bonnet near the nape of her neck.

"Oh, Jen, it's so beautiful and long. Don't. I miss mine; at least I think I do." Ellis ran her fingers along the strand and tucked it back in place. Jenny awkwardly patted Ellis's curls that peeked out beneath the cloche.

"No. We are stopping at the barber's in town. I'll get mine bobbed and we'll look just like sisters. Besides, I have my heart set on wearing that hat you have on." Jenny's eyes danced with a mischievous light that made Ellis laugh.

The young women pressed up the road as it rose before them, climbing now almost directly along the slope of the large hill. They turned the corner onto High Street; the much wider main road ran along the base of the hill, descending gently toward the town to the south. The dying leaves from the trees cascaded down around the road in the gentle breeze.

Suddenly Ellis stopped in the middle of the road.

"Ellis," Jenny asked, "what is it?"

The house was enormous, set back from the road and sur-rounded by large lawns that sloped around it down the hillside toward the harbor beyond. A wide porte cochere supported the northern side of the mansion while a rough stonework face and columns supported the steeply pitched gables of the roof. A round turret struck toward the sky on the corner of the home with the curve of a broader, squat turret beyond. There was a chilling aspect to the home as though someone had originally intended it to be charming, but somehow it had grown monstrously out of hand. It was four stories of curved glass windows, balconies and ostentation all striving for, and forever failing in, harmony. Worse, for Ellis, there was a familiarity to it like a nightmare just at the edge of wakeful thought and a lovely dream that had gone terribly wrong. She was both drawn to the place and repulsed by it at the same time.

The thought that this should be familiar to her made her shudder.

"That's the Norembega!" Jenny smiled, though perhaps not as brightly as before. "It is Merrick's home. I think it turned out wonderfully; don't you agree, Ellis?"

Ellis drew in a deep breath.

"Maybe we should call," Jenny said, brightening at the prospect.

Ellis shivered at the thought of approaching the house. "No, Jenny. You said our party today was to be a surprise. We wouldn't want to spoil it, would we?"

"No." Jenny hesitated. "I suppose not but—"

Ellis did not wait for any discussion. She quickly continued down the road, with Jenny having to catch up.

The truth was that Ellis had remembered something . . . something cold, dark and foul that was calling to her, whispering to her from underground. It remained just beyond memory and she could not decide if she wanted to recall it or not.

Ellis barely heard Jenny's prattle for some time. She duly noted the Three Sisters' Inn on the west side of High Street between the Norembega and the northern edge of Gamin. The Disir sisters operated the inn. According to Jenny, Nurse Finny was the eldest of the sisters. Ellis had no desire to pay a call at the inn if her younger sisters were anything like Finny.

"Gamin should never look like that," sighed Jenny.

Ellis looked up. She had not realized that they had reached the town. High Street had turned on to Main, but it seemed that half of the town on the right side of the street was a charred ruin of partial walls; its bricks were soot covered and its windows stared back at them from empty partial arches. In most places the burnt timbers and fallen roofs had been cleared away and there was even evidence of scaffolding going up and fresh lumber prepared to rebuild the lost buildings.

Storefronts that were now nothing more than black gaping maws and boarded-up windows were at odds with the crisp, clean perfection of shops on the opposite side of the street. Beyond the central intersection of the town, next to a small park, was the ashen husk of a church. There was less of it remaining than the other ruins, but Ellis could see that the pulpit still stood in the charred remains. There was no evidence of rebuilding at the church. Three soldiers stood in the park next to it, just looking at it. One of the soldiers caught Ellis's eye and tipped his hat to her.

"Don't look at him," Jenny warned. "He'll think we want to talk to him." Before Ellis could protest, Jenny grabbed her elbow and hurried her back down the street and into the barbershop.

The barber was astonished at the women coming into his establishment. Ellis thought it odd that she and Jenny appeared to be the only two customers. The barber stood from his chair, looking somewhat at a loss as to what to do with Jenny as she removed her hat and sat down in his chair. Despite his nervousness, he managed to do a credible job of copying Ellis's style, and thirty minutes later two young ladies left the astonished barber sweeping up Jenny's tresses. As the women exited the shop, Ellis removed her hat and offered it to Jenny. Jenny, in turn, proffered her bonnet to Ellis.

"Now I feel ready to reintroduce my cousin to the Nightbirds."

"And your cousin's hat, too?" Ellis drew her mouth into a demure pout, which melted into a grin. Jenny poked her in the ribs and laughed.

"Come on, Ellie; they are all waiting for us," said Jenny.

Ellis stopped. "All who are waiting for us?"

"Everyone. Well, everyone who matters."

Ellis didn't move. "Jenny, just for whom is this 'surprise' intended?"

"None of us could stand that the doctor wanted to keep

you confined to the house. It seemed ridiculous and a little mean."

"But I'm not sure I'm ready to meet a lot of people . . . especially people I am supposed to remember but obviously do not. Maybe we should just go home."

"Oh no, you don't! I'm wearing a stylish frock, hat and new hair. We are going to go make a splash down at the literary club. Besides, there will be an informal luncheon. You wanted to know more about Gamin and the people; well, here's your chance." Seeing Ellis hesitate, Jenny continued, "Please, Ellie, they planned it for you. Act surprised!"

Ellis understood that Jenny wanted to show off her new fashions to this "literary society" of hers at least as much as and probably more than she wanted to help her bewildered cousin. Jenny had concealed the fact that there was a planned gathering for Ellis. She let out a breath and realized she couldn't blame her. She would have stayed home if she had known it was a large party. She admitted inwardly that she might have done the same thing as Jenny. She fell into step alongside her cousin and they turned back up Main Street, past the shops on their right and the charred buildings on their left toward a brick building tucked back at the top of a small rise, which Ellis had not noticed on their way into town.

"See? It's just above the park. Just think. Maybe you will remember something."

Ellis singled out the stately redbrick building they were approaching. Geraniums and daisies bloomed in profusion in large pots flanking the tall front door. "So I have been to the literary society before?"

"Oh yes. I thought you understood. You see, you were—are quite a favorite. Everyone knows you there. You will be among friends."

Friends. Friends that I can't remember. She felt a weariness descend over her as she and Jenny climbed the front steps. "It's so kind of you to bring me here. Can we leave after lunch, though? I'm afraid I will be quite worn-out before we get home."

"Of course, Ellie. We don't want to upset the doctor!" Jenny winked at her and swung open the gleaming white door to the Nightbirds Literary Society.

The sound of the crowded hall poured out of the doorway, surrounding Ellis. She felt suddenly uncertain again, as there must have been nearly twenty people crowded into the space to welcome her.

"Oh, you're here. Finally!" Alicia, the young woman Ellis had met yesterday, rushed forward from the gaggle of young people. She was the other girl in the picture on Ellis's bed stand. Alicia took Ellis's arm and ushered her forward into a crowd of about two dozen young people. "Come in, come in. We are all so pleased you have returned to us. We are aching to know about—" Alicia faltered midsentence, not knowing how to finish.

"—the city," boomed a deep voice from the doorway. All faces turned in surprise toward the door. A shocked, anticipating silence fell on the room.

"Merrick! What a delight to see you here." Jenny's voice sounded more nervous than pleased. She turned on her heel so quickly that she stumbled awkwardly into the man's chest.

He stepped back and steadied her with his arm as he moved toward Ellis.

He looked around at the faces of the small crowd and said casually, "It seems that my invitation was misplaced. Well, no matter. I'm certain it was just an accidental oversight."

Silence reigned for a heartbeat before Alicia replied, "Of course it was. We couldn't get along without our founder." The exchange took the air out of the room.

"We won't spoil our first little reintroduction for Miss Harkington over such a trivial matter." He smiled, acknowledging Ellis and removing his hat. "Besides, I've brought my own surprise. Come in here, Elias, and join us!"

A young man of slight build stepped through the doorway, hat in his hand. His brown, curly hair held tightly to his head as though it had a will of its own. He had a slightly bug-eyed look and seemed uncertain, as though he wasn't confident about his welcome.

"Ely!" exclaimed Jenny. The group that surrounded her washed past Ellis to welcome the young man clapping and laughing, talking all at once. Relief and pleasure were on their faces. Ellis heard the word "fire" mingled with questions and tones of relief.

She observed that Merrick stood apart watching the others move around the young man, his face expressionless. "Enough about you, old chap. This party is to welcome back Miss Harkington and to reintroduce her to the Nightbirds."

"Yes, please come in all and sit down," said Alicia, who seemed to be the queen bee here. She led them all back down the hallway. There were closed doors to either side, but the group flowed through a set of doors at the end of the corridor and into a large wood-paneled room. Tall windows flanked a small stage set into the back wall, its curtain closed. Chairs had been set in a crescent on the polished oak flooring. Alicia was still piloting Ellis through the group, some of whom reached out furtively to touch her dress as she passed.

"Ellis, you sit here in the place of honor so that we can all see you." Alicia indicated an oversized ornately carved wooden chair that was the focal point of the room. It made Ellis think of a throne. Sitting on a throne seemed like something children would do, but she acknowledged a pleasurable sense of being allowed to sit in the place of honor, so she sat down in it. She felt nearly swallowed up in the chair's deep cushions. Her feet dangled near the floor. The skin near the neckline of her dress grew warm and heat rushed up into her cheeks. She couldn't decide if she was flushing from pleasure or embarrassment at so much attention. She looked about at her little court and felt something was missing, though she didn't know what it was. The rest of the party seated themselves in chairs and on floor cushions, bohemian-style, about the room.

Jenny brought a pillow for Ellis to rest her feet on and seated herself on a large brocade cushion next to the throne chair. Ellis was about to speak when Merrick stepped up to stand next to her, facing the group.

"As you know, one of our own has returned to us. But for her it is as though it were her first time." Merrick turned toward Ellis, his eyes intent and never leaving her face as he continued, "Let us all be considerate of that. Miss Harkington, welcome."

Ellis felt a disconcerted delight under the handsome man's gaze. She glanced down at Jenny, who gave no indication that she saw how pointedly Merrick looked at Ellis. Ellis was careful to smile and acknowledge each person in the group arrayed before her, avoiding Merrick's gaze.

"Thank you all," Ellis began tentatively. "You are all most kind to—"

"Tell us about the city!" said Alicia, and a rumble of approval rippled through the group.

Ellis swallowed, her heart skipping a beat. *What could I say, really? There was nothing but a gray fog, before the train ride here.*

"Yes!" called out a young man leaning anxiously forward on his chair. "Is it true that there is murder there? Tell us about murder!"

"Oh yes," cooed a plump young woman sitting in the front. "And diseases . . . and ecstasy. And cruelty! Is there cruelty in the city?"

"Yes, what about pleasure and silk?" asked a nodding barrel-chested man at the end of the row with a carefully trimmed mustache. "And fear . . . tell us about fear, by all means."

Ellis blinked, uncertain how to answer.

"Please," murmured Elias from the edge of the crowd, "tell us something of the city. Anything at all."

Ellis stared at the expectant faces looking back at her.

Merrick folded his arms across his chest, a smile playing about the edges of his lips.

Jenny leaped to her feet. "Here's something from the city! Come on, Ellie; let's show 'em." Jenny tugged at Ellis, who rose from the chair. Though Ellis didn't know what Jenny meant, a wave of relief washed over her as demanding eyes shifted from her to her cousin. "You know, the frocks," Jenny whispered over her shoulder.

The two young women turned a circle in place to the oohs and sighs of the other girls. Ellis felt a little silly modeling, especially in front of the young men, but it was much better than trying to talk about something she could not recall.

"And now, the finale! You ready, Ellie?" Jenny fingered the edge of her cloche with a gloved hand. Ellis smiled; she couldn't begrudge Jenny her chance to cause a splash. Ellis grasped the brim of her hat as well, and together they whisked the hats off.

Gasps and whisperings, giggles and coughing echoed around the room. "It's the latest from the city! Many young ladies are wearing bobbed hair." Jenny cupped the bouncy curls near the nape of her neck.

"I'm sure you both have caused a sensation and now all the young ladies will be getting a bob," said Alicia. Her tone lacked warmth. Ellis looked at the young women scattered about the room and noted disapproval on some of their faces. From the corner of her eye she glimpsed doubt sliding onto Jenny's features.

Ellis came to Jenny's rescue. "It's considered patriotic. Many women have bobbed their hair to work in the factories while the men are gone to war, and besides, it's so fun with the new dances." Ellis flipped her curls a little defiantly.

"Like what dances?" asked a young woman with bright green eyes and red hair.

"Like the Castle Walk or the turkey trot or even the

tango," announced Ellis. She caught Jenny's eye at the realization that she had just listed a number of things she had not
known two seconds before and it sent a shiver of delight up
her spine. She grasped the tips of her cousin's fingers and whispered, "I think I can dance." Jenny smiled and nodded. "I
wish there was a Victrola or something," whispered Ellis.

"Well, I think you'll probably get your wish," said Jenny,
smiling.

The room began to buzz loudly as young men leaped to
their feet and girls swished their skirts showing off whatever
steps they knew or thought they knew. Squeals and peals of
laughter rang out as they danced like a swarm of bees gone
mad.

"Say, here's a Victrola!" yelled a fellow wearing a bright
red blazer as he moved to the back of the hall.

Merrick's head snapped toward the voice. He glared, his
eyes fixed in astonishment on the machine.

Ellis could not remember seeing it when she first came in,
but now a new Victrola record player stood plainly near the
entrance door. She stepped up to it, admiring the shining
flower horn, the fresh felt on the turntable and the finish on
the case. A record case leaned against the table. Ellis reached
down and pulled out a glass gramophone from the sleeve. She
read the label and smiled. "Maple Leaf Rag," it read. She cen-
tered the gramophone on the spindle, cranked up the motor
and set the stylus on the outer area of the spinning disk.

The up-tempo music poured into the hall out of the Victrola's horn. Ellis stood in wonder as she watched everyone's
astonishment.

"What do we do now?" demanded Alicia over the tinny music.

"Well, you dance," Ellis said. "Most people dance a turkey trot to this music."

"In the city, right?" Jenny urged. "Show us, Ellie, please!"

The jaunty strains of the Joplin rag echoed throughout the large room.

"Well, I think it's something like this." Ellis pulled Jenny toward her, putting her in dance hold. "Hop on your left foot while raising the right knee, then up on the right foot while raising the left knee. Then you hop four times on your left foot with your leg out to the side while turning, then continue the turn while hopping on the right leg with the left leg held out to the . . ."

The Nightbirds in the room were already pairing off. Each couple was trying to dance the steps they had barely seen with enthusiastic abandon. The hall was a chaos of crazy motion, a mad caricature of a dance.

"Now you've done it." Jenny snickered lightly.

"No, you started it with that hair," said Ellis, grinning as she returned the tease.

Ellis's laughter faded into curiosity. She watched as Merrick stepped slowly toward the back of the hall, approaching the blaring record player as though it were a thing of menace. He stood for a long moment glowering at the cheerily playing device. He was reaching forward hesitantly to touch it as Ellis stepped up to him.

"Don't you care for the music, Mr. Bacchus?" Ellis chided.

Merrick jumped slightly as though startled but regained

his composure as he turned toward Ellis. "I am not accustomed to stepping out, Ellis, and not all things from the city have reached us here as yet. Tell me, did you happen to bring your book with you?"

"My book?" Ellis replied with a smile. "No, sadly, I did not bring a book. I was hoping I might borrow one . . . perhaps from this literary society."

Merrick gave her a quizzical look. "Indeed? You surprise me, Ellis."

"Do I?" Ellis said, tilting her head. "I can't imagine how."

The set of double doors on the far side of the Victrola swung wide open. Ellis turned at the sound. Beyond the open doorway was revealed one of the side rooms from the hall. A long, linen-covered table was set with plates of assorted foods.

Alicia clapped her hands together to gain some attention. "A light luncheon is now on the buffet, people. Please continue to enjoy yourselves." She strode into the side room, picked up a china plate from the buffet and, giving Jenny a baleful look, turned her back on the hubbub.

Jenny laughed, joining Ellis and Merrick. "Whatever Alicia commands must be obeyed!"

Merrick, a smile at the corner of his mouth, gestured Ellis and Jenny toward the side room.

A few dancers were attracted to the food. Ellis stood hesitantly, knowing it would be impolite to skip the luncheon in her honor. *Dancing.* She'd much rather dance than eat. She briefly glanced at Alicia's tightening lips, let out a small breath and politely headed for the buffet. The atmosphere in the side room was calm as people filled their plates. Ellis sat on a floor cushion next to the redheaded girl. Elias brought them lemonade and joined them. Jenny stood in the center of a small knot of admirers, who, ogling her hair, swept her back into the social hall, all of them begging for a dance. Jenny did not give Ellis even a backward glance that might have released her from the small predicament she was in. Alicia carefully shut the doors to the hall as the music was started up.

"I'm so glad you're back," said the redheaded girl. "You probably don't remember me, but I'm Martha. Things are always so lively when you're in charge."

"Really?" was all Ellis could think of to say. She was surprised by the comment. It was hard for her to imagine herself as a ringleader. And of course, this party was obviously Alicia's function, not hers. Besides, Ellis thought, it was Jenny who had set everyone off like firecrackers, wasn't it? Ellis took a bite of what turned out to be a bland cucumber sandwich and sipped nearly flavorless lemonade.

Elias sat quietly next to the girls and cast a furtive glance at Ellis. Martha, seeing it, said, "What is it, Ely? Do you want to ask Miss Harkington a question?"

"Well, if you don't mind, miss. Is it . . . wonderful in the city? What did you do there? Would we, I mean, I like it?"

Ellis pursed her lips together. She thought she had managed to neatly skirt the subject of where she was from, since she apparently had no more idea than this fellow what it was like there. She closed her eyes and hoped to make up something general that would satisfy him. A thin ribbon of images illuminated her inner vision. "There are tall storefronts, cobbled streets, an electric trolley, wool shops, seagulls and a port that is much larger than here."

"Ellis, are you finished with your plate?" Alicia hovered above her, Merrick at her back.

Ellis's eyes widened. She smiled. She had remembered something. Just a bit. She wasn't even certain the images she'd seen in her mind's eye were of where she was from, but it felt like a memory. Relief and giddiness filled her veins.

"Miss Harkington, Ellis, would you care to dance?" Merrick held out his hand to help her to her feet.

This was her chance to escape more questions she couldn't answer. "Thank you, I'd be delighted." She allowed him to help her up and as she did so caught the curious thundercloud look he shot Elias over her shoulder.

"We're going to dance." Merrick stated a fact. "Alicia, you should join us and let someone else clean up these plates."

"Gladly!" she said, and unceremoniously shoved the dirty plates onto the end of the buffet.

Ellis felt exhilarated as her heels clicked against the wooden dance floor and she was enveloped by the music. She found she could dance quite well. The dances were familiar to her feet. She loved it and Merrick was an adept partner. In fact, she knew just by the way they moved together that they must have danced together before. After three dances in a row she begged off and Merrick escorted her to a chair next to where Jenny was seated.

"Thank you." Ellis smiled gratefully up at Merrick. "You

rescued me back there at the luncheon. I didn't know what I was going to say to Ely. But I remembered, at least, think I remembered a few things. Anyway, thanks."

To Ellis's surprise, there was concern in his face. He whispered, "I hope you're OK and that the doctor won't be too put out with us for keeping you."

"Just a little tired. I'm going to be fine." As she said the word "fine" a wisp of hope lit in her heart. She had remembered a few things today.

"Maybe you should be on your way home before it gets too late in the day," he said.

"Oh, please let's dance for a while longer." Jenny looked up into Merrick's face and tossed her new short curls playfully with one gloved hand.

Merrick smiled a little hesitantly, but his voice was hearty: "Of course, Miss Jenny, you and I must have a turn about the floor."

"Or three!" she said pertly, winking at Ellis. Then Jenny gave him a pretty pout. "You haven't said anything about my new style."

Ellis was amazed to hear Jenny so brazenly fish for a compliment. Ellis looked at her hands and felt color creep into her cheeks.

"Dear Jenny, copies are seldom as good as the original." Jenny's face fell and Merrick pulled her away as the strains of a waltz began on the Victrola.

Ellis flushed beet red and found it difficult to stay in her chair. She struggled with the emotions of embarrassment and resentment. Embarrassed that Jenny was either so forward or so naïve that she didn't know what she had said was wrong. And Ellis resented Merrick's rude answer. She stole a glance at the pair gliding about the floor. By the smiles and words they were apparently exchanging while dancing one would never guess what had just passed between them. Ellis's emotions calmed. If neither of them was upset, why should she be distressed? *There is still so much I don't know,* she thought.

Ellis finally knew what it was that she felt was missing from the party as she held court among the Nightbirds: a chaperone. The inappropriateness of the situation was apparent to her. She suddenly felt very tired.

She sat through a number of melodies. It was most likely only a few minutes, but it felt like hours, and she was a little wounded that no one else had asked to partner her and she stared studiously at the floor. She started when Jenny grabbed her hands. "Come on. We're going down to the harbor to go home! A little sunset voyage, Ellie. It'll be fun."

Jenny held Ellis's arm tightly while pushing against the crush who were all trying to exit at once. The excited crowd poured out the side door of the hall, laughing and bumping shoulders while the Victrola loudly blared out "The Bumble Bee Rag."

"Shouldn't someone stop the music?" Ellis asked Jenny over the din.

"Don't worry about it! It'll be fine." Jenny shrugged and dove outside into the crowd.

Ellis wondered briefly if there were silent, unseen servants who would clean up the luncheon room and hall after the

young people's departure. Jenny had been right, Ellis mused.
It seemed no one would ask her to read a book. She hadn't
seen bookshelves, let alone books, that afternoon at the Nightbirds Literary Society.

8

SPYGLASS

The late-afternoon air was warm as the party swarmed up the street toward a small dock where several dinghies, sporting jaunty little sails, were tied up. Ellis's step slowed as she approached the water and wondered who owned these little boats. Hesitation crawled up her spine.

Jenny steered Ellis toward the boat that Merrick and Alicia had just boarded. The little boat bobbed in the water against the dock. He held up his hand. Jenny took it and gingerly stepped aboard. Ellis looked out across the ripples of the Persian blue water. A sense of dread welled up in her and her breathing became shallow.

"I don't like going out on the water, do I?" she asked Merrick.

"It's quite safe, I assure you, Ellis," he answered.

"Yes, but I don't like going out on the water, do I?"

"Jenny, it seems your guest has remembered something about her former life." Merrick turned to Jenny, who had seated herself. She was looking off to sea and didn't respond.

"It's all right. Why don't you all go have your sunset sail around the bay? I can walk home." Ellis hoped the weariness she felt didn't show.

Ellis stood awkwardly on the rough wooden planks of the dock, knowing that Jenny must want to sail away with Merrick, and was equally certain she could not voluntarily get into the boat.

"Don't fret, dear Ellis; I'll be happy to drive you home, if you like." Merrick stepped onto the dock.

It was the second time he'd saved her that afternoon. Ellis's breathing deepened. She smiled and graciously nodded her thanks.

"Well, we'll all go in the car then. If you don't mind two more, Merrick?" said Alicia as Merrick helped her from the boat.

"Come along, Jenny." Merrick held out his hand to the last occupant on the boat. His mild tone belied his stern face. Jenny, without looking up, stood and allowed him to assist her onto the quay. She gave Ellis a cold little glance as she walked past her. Merrick turned and waved off the rest of the party as they headed out for their cruise.

"My automobile is just around the corner from the society house." Merrick fell into stride next to Ellis. "Things being what they are, young ladies shouldn't be out walking unescorted."

Jenny, two strides ahead of them, turned her head. "You let me walk into town and back by myself yesterday, Mr. Bacchus." She tossed the words over her shoulder, not looking back.

"Yes, I'm sorry I wasn't able to help you. The train arrived a bit later than we thought it would. Anyway, Jenny, you know it's a new day and some of us are worried that trouble could come, has come, to Gamin. In fact, I don't think it's quite right that two unprotected young women should be out on the point by themselves."

Listening to him, Ellis agreed wholeheartedly. The living arrangements at Summersend were quite odd. But what was to be done? she wondered.

"You know, ladies, there is a great deal more room at the Norembega than either the doctor or I ever use. You could have the entire third floor to yourselves. I would feel better knowing that you are under my protection."

Ellis blinked and looked wide-eyed at the sidewalk. Had he just suggested that she and Jenny live in his home? Did she mistake what he was saying? She tried, but she couldn't make anything of it other than that which she had heard. She might have forgotten her previous life but not the rules of decent living. She had come to understand that Gamin was a place of strange sensibilities: no aunt or uncle at Summersend and no chaperone at the Nightbirds House. But now this proposal to live under a bachelor's roof? It was too much. Young single ladies did not live with bachelors.

"No, thank you, Mr. Bacchus—"

Ellis's quietly controlled answer was drowned out by Jenny's reply.

"That would be perfect!"

Merrick clapped his hands together and smiled broadly. "Wonderful. I'll be around to get your luggage this—"

"*No!*"

Everyone stared at Ellis in her vehemence.

"I'm sorry. What you suggest is quite impossible." The words exploded as they escaped Ellis's stiff lips.

"Merrick has offered us a great kindness, Ellie. What's the matter?" Jenny's tone was surprised and hurt.

Merrick silently scrutinized Ellis's face, apparently waiting for her reply. Ellis wondered if it was possible none of her companions could see how wrong it would be. She looked questioningly at Alicia's face but saw there only a veiled pensiveness and the girl would not meet her eyes. Ellis let out a long, slow breath, realizing that she simply did not fully understand the situation she'd been cast into.

"May we discuss this at home, Jenny?"

"Fine."

Merrick looked back at the little boats on the bay. Alicia kept pace with the two cousins but volunteered nothing.

They reached Merrick's automobile without further discussion. It was a four-door hardtop Cadillac: a Type 55 Touring Model. Merrick turned to help each of the ladies into the vehicle, but Jenny charged past him. She opened the door and, stepping onto the running board and into the car, seated herself on the passenger's side. Merrick said nothing but simply helped Ellis and Alicia into the backseat before taking his place behind the wheel. He inserted a key into the ignition, switched it to on, set the choke on the dash panel and pressed down on the starter. The engine sputtered and chugged to life, smoothing out as Merrick adjusted the spark to adjust the engine timing.

"As you can see, Ellis," Merrick commented, "I've a few toys of my own."

Merrick adjusted the spark and advanced the throttle in the center of the steering wheel as he released the clutch. The automobile lurched slightly into gear and then accelerated smoothly as it turned onto High Street.

"Alicia," Merrick said, turning his head back slightly to address his passengers in the backseat. "What were you telling me about that scrapbook page you were working on earlier?"

Alicia stiffened next to Ellis. "I'm sure Miss Harkington doesn't want to hear about—"

"I wanted to hear more about it," Merrick prodded. "I'm sure it will be perfectly all right so far as Ellis is concerned."

"Well, it's . . . it's really going to be wonderful," Alicia said, her voice growing more wistful as she spoke. "There will be a carousel with white horses, each one with eyes of brilliant jewels. I've put a lion tamer on the page and dozens of stalls and wagons on a wide midway. Each one will be filled with games and freaks and curiosities. There's a fat lady and a strongman and a clown tent. There's even a fortune-teller. Oh, and all kinds of thrilling rides."

"It sounds like you've put a lot of thought into it," Merrick commented.

"It will all be put in a sunset park," Alicia said with quiet longing. "I've used felt pieces for the most part, but some of the sky is out of satin. Everyone will be there—I've even put Ellis on the page."

"How very nice," Merrick said casually. "And what about you, Ellis? How is your scrapbook coming along?"

"My scrapbook?" Ellis was puzzled.

"Yes," Merrick said. "Have you made any changes to it?"

"Oh, I don't have a scrapbook," Ellis said.

Jenny kept her eyes fixed sullenly on the dashboard in front of her, but Alicia turned her head sharply toward Ellis in surprise. "You don't? Then how did you ever manage to—"

"Alicia, I think we've shared quite enough," Merrick said in a firm voice. "We've put Ellis through a great deal today."

Alicia stopped speaking at once. She turned away from Ellis, staring silently out the side window of the car.

Ellis felt tired and heartsick. She reasoned with herself that she should not feel she had spoiled the afternoon. She had been reasonable. She surmised from the attitude of her companions that she was the only one here who thought so. Ellis gazed at the lush pink and blue sunset that surrounded them, wishing she could have forced her feet into the little boat and that she was sailing carefree around the bay with the other Nightbirds. She swallowed hard. It wasn't just her past she knew nothing about. Her knowledge of the present felt like a game of blindman's bluff that she was playing with eyes wide open. Her mind filled with more questions than ever, she found a longing for the privacy of her room at Summersend.

.   .   .

When they arrived home Jenny slipped from the car and ran inside without even thanking Merrick. Merrick set the hand brake and stepped around the car to open Ellis's door.

"Thank you for the luncheon, Alicia. I feel very welcomed by everyone," Ellis said, turning back to Alicia. Ellis felt the awkwardness of Jenny's rudeness and paused a few heartbeats before adding, "I'm sorry, I just don't understand anything, you know."

Alicia's look softened. "Jenny was considering being Merrick's intended before . . . well, before the accident. They were good together back then. It only seems fitting that he should watch over her during the troubles."

Ellis permitted Merrick to help her out of the car. He followed her up the steps of Summersend to the door. Pausing a moment on the porch, he suddenly snatched up Ellis's hand, kissing it.

"Good night, sweet Ellie," he said quietly. "Do you dream?"

Ellis smiled. It was a lovely and odd question.

"Please consider my offer," he whispered. "I gather it seems extraordinary to you. But considering what you have been through, it may be necessary for all our sakes." His demeanor was earnest and kind. She felt he meant her no disrespect or harm in his offer.

"Thank you. I promise that Jenny and I will discuss it." Ellis returned the gentle pressure of his hand before turning to go into the house.

Ellis was not the only one longing for her room. Jenny was

nowhere to be found on the ground floor of the house. After a cursory walk through the garden, Ellis guessed Jenny had done what Ellis also wished to do: taken refuge in her own room. They would speak later.

Ellis climbed the stairs to her room. She was surprised to find everything neatly organized. No clothes or shoes were strewn about as she'd left them. The room had been aired and dusted, the mirror polished. The curtains were drawn back from the French doors and the light from the sun now low on the horizon gleamed like red liquid fire on the waters of the bay. She started to question the "who and how" of her room being rearranged in her absence, but weariness wrapped its sleepy arms about her and for a moment she quit questioning and chose to simply feel grateful. She lay down on her bed and gave way to the relief of weeping.

When she had cried herself out she pushed her curls away from her face and stood up, brushing her crumpled dress with her hands.

During the torrent of tears a thought had broken like a lightning storm in her mind: *What if I don't really belong here at all? What if someone out there, beyond Gamin, is looking for me?*

Alarm spread to her limbs. Rummaging through her closet, she found an overnight case. She opened a dresser drawer and savagely stuffed the little case with clothing. She began forming a plan, a plan to leave. She'd been brought to this place, but she didn't have to stay. It occurred to her that if she could just get to the train station she could leave. She pinched her fingers trying to close the too-full case as she realized she would need a train ticket. She grabbed her little purse and emptied it. No money. She looked through the dresser drawers, the pockets of her green traveling suit and then her trunk. The search yielded no paper money, nor any coins. Her legs weakened and she sat down on the bed, shoving at the overnight case that obligingly slid to the floor with a satisfying thud. Her hands shook.

She felt physically ill as fatigue swept over her body. *If I left this place which way should I go? And how would I explain who I am when I got there?* She was homesick for a place and people she couldn't remember.

The doctor hasn't said it, nor the nurse or Jenny or Merrick, but it is in their eyes; they all think I'm not quite right—that I am frail in body and spirit.

The world no longer makes sense and I am too weak to leave this place. She was filled with a mountain of unanswered questions that felt unscalable. She closed her eyes against the pink light of sunset as a few tears of defeat fell and then dried upon her cheeks. She chose not to sleep.

She realized she disliked napping at sunset. She plucked up this thought and held it like a small, precious diamond.

At least that's one more thing I know about myself. I'll gather all my pieces together yet, she thought.

She heard a door open down the hallway and footsteps on the stairs. She sat up and slipped on her shoes. She knew that she and her cousin needed to discuss Merrick's rather scandalous offer from this afternoon and they had avoided it long enough.

Ellis slipped back downstairs. She could not see where Jenny had gone, but her eye caught something new resting behind the bell jar on the table down the hall.

It was a sheet of music.

Ellis was drawn to it. She picked it up and smiled as she read the title. *Jenny must have put this here for me,* she thought. *A peace offering.*

With relief, Ellis moved quickly into the music room. She settled onto the piano bench, placed the sheet music before her, set her hands to the keys and began to play.

The keys responded to her hands. Music flowed from the instrument and into the house. Ellis felt the ecstasy of the motion and the sound, peace flowing into her like cool water quenching a desert thirst.

"It's beautiful," Jenny said quietly from behind Ellis.

"Yes, it is." Ellis smiled as she played. "And I am most grateful for it. Thank you, Jenny."

"Oh, but it isn't from me," Jenny said, her voice at once guarded.

Ellis faltered through a measure. *If it isn't from Jenny, then where did it come from?* Ellis concentrated on the notes before her, the music spinning perfection into the room once more. It had brought them both to talking again, which was the important thing at the moment. "Never mind. I'm talking nonsense."

"What is it?" Jenny asked.

"The music?"

"Yes."

"It says its Liszt's Liebestraum number three." Ellis nodded.

"I'm sure I've played this before, but I feel like I'm hearing it for the first time."

The music flowed around them for a moment, filling the silence.

"We used to play the most beautiful duets together." Jenny sighed. "You and I."

Ellis stopped, drawing her hands away from the keyboard. Silence fell between them.

"I'm so sorry, Jenny," Ellis said. "We should have stayed home, as the doctor asked."

"No, Ellis," Jenny said, looking away. "I should have trusted you."

Jenny held her arms tightly across her chest, her head bowed as she stepped back out of the room. Ellis followed Jenny out onto the back porch and breathed in the early-evening air.

"Jenny?" she said gently, crossing to the girl.

Jenny was leaning against the porch railing gazing out over the water. She turned a tear-streaked face to Ellis and whisked the tears away with the back of her hand. "I'm sorry, too, Ellis. It's all so confusing."

Ellis nodded and looked at the painted planks of the porch in the gathering dusk. "What Merrick offered this afternoon, it's not right. You understand why I said no, don't you?"

"I don't know. I guess so. Ellis, you know that he is supposed to be mine. Did you see how much attention he pays to Alicia and, now, to you? Everything was different before . . . before." She held up her crippled hand and dropped it by her side.

Ellis began to comprehend that Jenny's poor mood was

about more than a spoiled sunset cruise. She had noticed Merrick's attentions to Alicia and herself. Ellis had seen a gentle pity in Merrick's eyes when speaking with Jenny today. And it was pity, not the ardent carefulness of a suitor. If he bore Jenny more feeling than that, Ellis had not seen it this afternoon. And she could not remember life beyond it. To her eyes, he behaved like any unattached male. She had no way to advise Jenny. Ellis admitted in her heart she had enjoyed dancing with him today and the way they had moved so easily together. It was a bit of the unremembered but familiar. Ellis wondered briefly if Jenny had made more of Merrick's past courtesies than she should. Ellis brushed this thought aside, realizing that it had sprung to life as a hope.

"I'm sorry, Jenny. I'll—"

"You'll what? Make him pay attention to me?" Jenny's words were clipped as she turned back to the railing. "Maybe we—you—should reconsider his offer."

Ellis exhaled, considering her words. "I won't deny that the stories in the papers are unsettling. I find it . . . unusual that we are out here in this large house alone. Are there no older people we could stay with or who would come here? Perhaps we could go to my relations in the city until the culprit is caught."

Jenny reasoned aloud, "You can't go home right now and I can't imagine who in Gamin would welcome us. The Disir sisters, perhaps. But you have already met Finny and the other two are as peculiar as their sister. They are fine company for afternoon tea, but more than that? No. Gamin is suddenly different now that trouble is so close by. It could come here, Ellis.

This is the first time I have ever felt unsafe at Summersend. It's my haven, you know. It's all I have, really. I wish you would reconsider Merrick's offer. I'm sure it is kindly meant. And it might just give me a chance. . . ."

Ellis realized that in her present state she felt alone and vulnerable and would like a champion to lean on. But she had to tread on that thought carefully. Now that she glimpsed Jenny's feelings for Merrick, she was unprepared physically and mentally to engage in this conversation.

"I'll think about it; I promise." She knew it was a poor answer but breathed out the relief of letting it go.

"If trouble comes to Gamin"—Jenny smiled tentatively and squared her shoulders as she walked to the back door—"then the matter will be out of our hands."

"Careful what you wish for," Ellis chided. Jenny's desire seemed childish and a little frightening. For her part, Ellis ardently wished for peace.

The golden beam from the lighthouse on the island in the bay splayed itself across the water in the misty blue evening light. She leaned against the porch railing, one hand reaching out as she steadied herself against it.

Her hand met with a cylindrical object. . . .

A spyglass.

She picked it up and, extending it out, placed her eye to it.

She found the beam upon the water and followed it back to the lighthouse and the brightly lit little cottage adjacent to it. To her surprise she saw a woman carrying a basket near the cottage. It was the same size as the one the baby had been in. She wondered about the nurse's mysterious little companion.

The expanse of her vision widened. Ellis felt as though she were being pulled through the lens of the spyglass to the little scene. She was disappointed as the woman put the basket down at the foot of a wash line and began pulling in linens that had blown dry in the afternoon breeze. No baby. As the woman worked, a little boy tugged at her skirts and scampered about, his hair blowing in the ocean air. Ellis saw that he was chasing large pink moths that were attracted by the cottage lights and, no doubt, the beam of the lighthouse itself. He chattered and romped, trying to coax the flitting beauties into his hands. After the woman filled her basket the little fellow came to her. She swung him around high in the air. Ellis smiled, thinking she could hear the sound of his laughter as he flew in his mother's arms. Ellis felt as though she'd been drawn into their small scene and that she stood only a few feet from them. The woman then tucked the basket under one arm and took the boy's hand. Together they opened the cottage door. Light spilled out and was quickly gone.

Ellis ached to knock on the door and join them.

A sudden gust of wind whipped about her, pushing her slightly off balance. She recovered at once, lowering the spyglass as she gripped the rail and was once again on the porch at Summersend, alone.

A black storm was driving across the waters of Penobscot Bay. Lightning flashed behind the veil of dark and menacing clouds.

The little island in the bay seemed serene and untouchable by the outside world. Ellis collapsed the spyglass and felt renewed shame in being unable to get into the little boat that afternoon. The cottage at the lighthouse seemed to hold all that Ellis's heart desired. She longed for home, family, laughter, peace and the memory to go with it all. The evening air was chill, stirring into a gale as she went inside.

"The storm is coming," she said as she latched tight the door behind her.

9

WRECK OF THE *MARY CELESTE*

Capt. Isaiah Walker staggered out of the woods to the shoreline. The storm had called him out of his hiding place like a siren. Through the driving rain and the roll of thunder somehow he sensed more than heard the banshee keening of the wind through the rigging of a ship in trouble at sea.

The beam of the Curtis lighthouse flashed through the gale on his right, the sweep of its brilliant rays cutting through the tempest. At first Isaiah saw nothing but the sheets of water cascading down from the angry darkness overhead and the lace-like spindrift whipped from the capping waves in the bay.

The captain tried to keep his feet under him in the rain. The ship was out there. He could feel her in his bones, struggling against the storm, desperate for the harbor and home.

He knew because he had been there, too.

Capt. Isaiah Walker was not actually a captain in any offi-cial capacity of the word, though everyone in the town called him that and, indeed, most of the inhabitants believed him to be of that rank. He had arrived in Gamin under circum-stances that he had never fully explained. His dark, weary eyes with the glint of desperation looked with a piercing gaze from over his baggy lower eyelids and the drooping of his hound-dog face. He styled his narrow beard along the edge of his jaw and chin, an extension of his sideburns. His hair was always neatly trimmed—"too neat for a seaman," those in the town murmured among themselves in disapproval of his af-fection.

He did not care for or seek their approval or their com-pany. He longed only to leave the mistakes of his past behind and think upon which wind he should follow next. He did not know where he was going, but he certainly knew the way by which he had come and dreaded that it might be happen-ing once again.

The captain tried to steady his footing on the rocky shore, the soles of his boots shifting on the uncertain ground. His peacoat was soaked, as was the broad-brimmed hat both held and tied firmly to his head. He peered again out from the shore.

She was there. He knew it.

He could hear the scream of the wind through her rigging, cutting above the roar of the storm and the crashing waves against the shore. He had to do something. Had to somehow stop the calamity, although he realized in that moment he had no real means to do so. He reached up and wiped the pouring sheets of rain from his face and looked again into the darkness.

The beam of Curtis Light again swept over the water, its shaft cutting through the darkness in its path.

"There!" the captain cried out with a start, his words swallowed immediately by the gale. "There she is!"

He had only glimpsed her in the swift beam from the lighthouse, but he took her all in at a glance. A schooner, three masted and gaff rigged. Her sails, however, were in tatters, their shreds flailing from the yards. She had heeled over, too, perhaps as far as twenty degrees on her starboard side. Her gunnels were close to the waterline and she rolled sluggishly with the waves.

"She's lost headway and her rudder," the captain murmured to himself. "She'll founder for sure."

Lightning cut across the sky just as the lighthouse beam flashed past the scene once more. The bow had shifted with the wind to starboard, rolling the ship heavily on her port side. The brilliance of the lightning flash blinded him for a moment. He reached up once more, wiping the water from his face, then stared again into the darkness.

The lighthouse beam again swung past.

The captain's eyes grew suddenly wide with fear.

The waves along the shore had caught the hull of the schooner, driving her toward shore in concert with the wind. In a moment the bow was surging with the waves directly toward the spot where the captain stood onshore. The bowsprit was already rushing over him, the masts towering above as lightning erupted in the clouds directly overhead.

The captain leaped aside, hurling his body out of the way of the onrushing bow. The bow smashed against the rocks, splintering and groaning as the waves caught the side of the hull, carrying it against the shore. Isaiah clawed at the wet sand, struggling to get his footing as the hull rolled menacingly toward him with the surf. The stern cracked against the jutting rocks, water pouring through the gaping hole into the stern bilge. The ship groaned again, the stern settling firmly into the sand just offshore as the aft hull filled with water. The hull settled backward, nearly righting itself for the last time as the schooner grounded, her keel broken.

Isaiah lay with his back against the sand, staring up at the awful scene. The tangle of masts, stays, ratlines and flapping canvas shreds he could see now only in silhouette against the turn of the lighthouse beam from the other side of the point. He perceived the vague outlines of the ship's name on the prow above him, but he could not make it out in the darkness. The wind shrieked through the taut rigging, an assault on his ears that was like a siren's call to death.

Isaiah pushed himself up off the sand quickly, peering through the driving storm. He cupped his hands to his mouth, calling out against the raging wail around him, "Ahoy! Ahoy there! Ahoy!"

Just like before, he thought. *But there is something different this time . . . something has changed.*

He glanced up and down the shore. The captain certainly did not expect to see anyone out on such a violent night. He had only come because something about the ship had called him. Yet he wished that someone was here—anyone—who might somehow take the burden of the captain's knowledge from him and let him sink back into obscurity.

That was when he saw the man.

He was lying facedown on the shore. He wore a long coat over wide shoulders and was struggling to push himself up from the sand. Even as the captain watched, the man collapsed back down, his boots milling in the silt without effect.

The captain rushed toward the man, kneeling at his side. He turned the figure over. In the darkness, however, it was impossible to see any details of the man's face beyond a frighteningly dark stain that could be seen covering his forehead and right eye. "Easy, mate! You're ashore now."

"I . . . I made it," the man coughed.

"Aye, you made it, though I don't rightly know how many others were as fortunate." Isaiah nodded. He glanced up the black side of the hull toward the deck above him. The lines continued to shift and the ragged sail canvas snapped and flailed in the tempest, but he could see no movement of any crew. "I'll just take a look about for your mates and see how they be faring. You seem to be in one piece after all. You stand fast right here until I get back."

The man nodded his ascent, rolling away from Isaiah to face away from him lying on the sand.

The captain stood up and turned his attention back to the ship. The waves continued to crash about the hull, but the timbers were barely moving. Isaiah knew she was grounded solidly and would be going nowhere for quite some time—if ever again. Several of the ship's rigging lines had come loose and now hung over the side. Isaiah tested several and found them shifting free but on his fifth attempt discovered a line that was secured to the deck rail. With practiced ease he used the rope to clamber up the side of the hull. He swung his legs over the gunnel and set foot on the slanting deck.

The deck was littered with debris but deserted. A forward transom was completely dark inside. The main cargo hatch was tightly battened into place, although he could see the pronounced buckling of the deck on either side of the hatch where the ship's keel had snapped. Farther back Isaiah spotted a flickering light swinging beyond the portholes of the cabin transom, but not a single crewman was on deck. The helm twisted eerily on its own on the poop deck.

"It's just the waves working the rudder," Isaiah reminded himself, but the absence of a crew unnerved him. "It's just part of the game is all."

"Hallo!" the captain yelled into the raging storm as he stepped back carefully along the deck toward the stern, feeling his booted footfalls beneath him. He was more cautious still where the deck planking was buckled. The bent and snapped planks were the surface sign of more mortal wounds to the ship beneath his feet and the deck was less certain here. At last he slipped past the hatch cover to the aft transom. There was a short gangway down to the closed doors of the cabin.

"Hallo!" he shouted again just as lightning tore the clouds overhead and the thunder drowned him out.

The deck suddenly shifted beneath his feet. A shiver ran up Isaiah's spine. He reached for the latch on the cabin doors and pulled them open. Yellow light spilled out from the hatch and he quickly stepped inside.

The howling was muted in the cabin. Isaiah recognized the salon at once. Hurricane lamps rocked back and forth in their suspended mounts, their wicks carefully trimmed and burning brightly. There was a long table mounted to the floor that ran almost the length of the compartment. Chairs were strewn about from the motion of the storm and the collision with the shore.

It was the smell that took him aback. He had never encountered such sensations before. Plates of food were strewn about the cabin, cooked meats, bread, cheese and fruits all tumbled to a mash on the floor. Isaiah reached down and touched a piece of ham on the floor. It was still warm to the touch.

"Hallo there!" Isaiah called out. "Anyone aboard?"

He straightened up and ran his hand down his face both to get the water away from his eyes and as an act of hesitation. He set his teeth and stepped quickly around the table to the darkened hallway beyond. Flashes from the storm came through the transom windows but did not penetrate the corridor well. Isaiah bit at his lip and then stepped into the dark passageway.

"I'm Isaiah Walker!" he called out, his own voice sounding muffled in his ears. He kept talking as much for his sake as for any other ears that might hear him. "You've run aground and I've come to help. Happened to meself once—so I know what you're facing."

He paused in the passage. The kitchen to his left was warm and he could see the glow from behind the stove grating. The fire had been banked properly.

A dim glow to his left outlined the edges of a passageway door. He fumbled for a moment for the handle and opened it.

It was a passenger cabin, a single candle in its lantern shielding it. The space was typically cramped. There was a trunk and a pair of cases stacked on the floor. The upper case was open. Several dresses were carefully packed in the case, with a long print dress laid out on the bunk next to it.

In the corner of the bunk rested a porcelain doll, its head cracked and missing a piece from its forehead down over its left eye. A baby rattle sat next to it atop a crumpled soft blanket.

"Passengers, and women at that," Isaiah muttered to himself. He took the candle from the lamp glass and stepped back into the corridor. Another door lay at the end of the hall. He felt a sudden urgency and stepped quickly to open the last door.

It was the captain's cabin in the style of the schooners, cramped and efficient. Captains of such vessels were meant to be on deck, not holed up in their cabins. Under the flickering candlelight Isaiah saw that the captain's cap was resting on his bunk along with his weather gear.

The logbook lay open on the small table, the quill dripping ink where it lay abandoned on the desk out of the inkpot. Isaiah moved the candle closer. Isaiah reached for the book with care and slowly flipped over the cover so that he could read its title.

LOG OF THE *MARY CELESTE*
Capt. Joseph Aarons Commanding

Isaiah laid the book flat again and peered down at the words written in a tight and precise hand on the page:

SEPTEMBER 6TH, 1917: Set sail 8:45 am out of Halifax, Nova Scotia, bound for Moncton, N.B. Crew of six, passengers: Mr. and Mrs. Mont-Blanc and child; Miss Julia Carter; Miss Hepseba Lindt. With officers fourteen souls aboard.

SEPTEMBER 7TH, 1917: Arrived Moncton, N.B. Provisioned and trade. Disembarked Miss Carter. Took on shipment steam engine parts. Set sail 2:35 pm bound for St. John. Weather turning foul. Following wind making good time despite high seas.

SEPTEMBER 8TH, 1917: Arrived St. John early, 5:45 am. Off-loaded steam engine parts. Departure of Miss Hepseba Lindt. Took on passenger Miss Philida Epstein and no cargo. Departure 1:15 pm bound for Bar Harbor.

SEPTEMBER 9TH, 1917: Swells and a southern wind. Progress slow. Unable to make St. John, weathering at sea.

SEPTEMBER 10TH, 1917: Entered St. John, N.B., harbor 9:10 am. Disembarked Miss Epstein 10:30 am. No new passengers. Took on cargo of wool packets. Minor repairs. Provisions and departure at 4:50 pm bound for Penumbra, Maine.

SEPTEMBER 11TH, 1917: Weather worsening. Following seas driving us toward shore. Unable to outrun the storm. Hatches secured. We are making for Curtis Light and will weather in Gamin Harbor. Curtis Light in sight. . . .

"Curtis Light in sight," Isaiah muttered, his brows knotted in a question. "Where are they, then? Where have they all gone?"

Isaiah glanced up at the top of the writing desk.

A pipe lay in its holder, the tobacco still smoldering and its smoke curling up from the bowl carved with the initials "J.A." on its side.

Isaiah took in a shuddering breath. The ship felt suddenly close, its air stifling.

Then he remembered the man on the beach.

Isaiah rushed from the cabin and down the corridor. He plunged out of the salon through the doors and out onto the deck. The full force of the storm had not abated and struck him as he skidded onto the wet, sloping deck. He tripped in his haste to cover the length of the debris-laden planks, felt the ship groan again beneath him and came at last to the railing. Without hesitation he gripped the rope, moving too quickly down its wet length and losing his grip. He fell heavily onto the sand and staggered to his feet.

"Sir! Might I have a word with you about—"

Isaiah could see the impression in the sand, filling with the deluge of rainwater from the sky, where the man had lain.

But the man was now gone.

"An outsider," Isaiah muttered into the storm. "Just like me."

10

OBSCENITY

With no appetite for food or company Ellis softly climbed the stairs and silently shut the door to her room. *Perhaps I will awaken knowing everything again,* she mused. Hope lit momentarily in her soul and passed on like the lighthouse beam that passed over her form through the windows of the French doors that overlooked the harbor. *If not,* she promised herself, *there will be adequate daylight to shine on all the mysteries in the morning.*

She wearily tugged the sheer curtain panels from beneath the heavy velvet ones across the glass doors. The wash of light from the lighthouse was softer and diffused as it spilled across the room followed by its withdrawal. Its slow but regular pulse was soothing, much like an ocean tide in its ceaseless rhythm. Outside, the storm had broken over Summersend. The wind rattled the panes, moaning as it picked up and swirled around the gingerbread ornaments under the eaves. Still the constant pulse of the lighthouse was calming to her. Weariness fell over her. She took off her shoes and silk stockings, lay down across the bed and fell asleep before she finished undressing.

She became aware of the sound of a persistent tapping against the French doors. Moths fluttered against the panes of glass, their silhouettes creating patterns against the organza sheers. They were a shadowy kaleidoscope, ornate and exotic, bobbing and weaving against the glass.

Moths in the storm? Ellis could not comprehend it. The gale outside was accompanied by the hiss of driving rain against the windowpanes. The latch gave way and in an instant the doors flew open. The banshee keening of the wind filled the room.

The darkness around her bed fluttered. Ellis's heart skipped a beat as she sat up and the night shattered into a thousand dark wings.

Wings gently caressed her neck, brushed her hands and skimmed along her eyelashes. She strained her eyes to see, peering into the darkness of her bedroom. The French doors lay open and without warning the blinding beam of the lighthouse lit the room like lightning. She closed her eyes and reopened them. The lighthouse beam slowed in its traverse and spilled across the floor. She was not alone. Hundreds of moths with wings of silky black and luminescent surrounded her. Delicately, gently, they slid in the air about her. Terror and excitement warred in her breast as she watched the graceful winged creatures. She could not help but think of the little boy chasing the pink moths. But these things had come to her.

She tried to cry out for help, but as she opened her mouth a moth flew in, and she inhaled and she swallowed it. She gagged, coughed and struggled for air. Her stomach felt as though it would lose its contents. She sat shivering, though she wasn't cold. She parted her lips to scream but could not utter a sound.

Her unwelcome visitors became larger and larger, crowding her room, beating her with their huge wings, sucking out the air. Ellis struggled to take a breath. She covered her eyes as the lighthouse beam canvassed her room. She looked up and the moths had gathered into a single form. It enfolded itself tightly in its huge black wings. The wings fell back as a many-layered greatcoat. A male form became clearly outlined, darkness against the moonlight now streaming through the window at his back. His silhouette was tall, with broad shoulders and slender hips. The ribbons upon his chest glistened in the moonlight, head bent low, face hidden in the shadows.

A soldier.

He closed the French doors against the storm, then strode forward and knelt at her bedside, where she sat huddled in the coverlet. Her heart pounded so that she thought it would burst from her chest.

"Ellis . . ."

He whispered her name simply and yet there was a rushing wind in his breath that spoke of green summer, bitter winter, resigned autumn and a thousand glorious springs.

Ellis licked her lips but still could not utter a sound.

"Dear Ellis." He sighed. "Do you know me?" She could

see the set of his jawline was earnest in the darkness. Almost imperceptibly she shook her head no.

"I am yours, Ellis. . . . I have always been yours." He knelt by her bedside and gently slid one hand up the coverlet, clasping in it both of her hands, which were clinging to the quilt. Ellis stared at the hand that held both of hers. He had long, tensile fingers. The pads of his fingertips were roughened as though he was no stranger to work. His strong hands were warm against her cold skin. "I came for you as I promised I would."

Ellis trembled, trying to speak.

"Be mine again, dear Ellie." He proffered a single white rose that he laid across her coverlet. As the lighthouse outlined their forms he held up his head and faced her. The flash of fire in his large gray-green eyes caused her throat to constrict with longing for something, something she didn't quite understand or remember. It seemed as though a memory belonging to her played deeply in those wonderful eyes. Her gaze fell to his mouth as a small sigh escaped his lips. He leaned in and slipped his arm about her waist, pulling her into his chest. Tilting his head down, he took possession of her lips, kissing her mouth slowly, deeply, knowingly. Ellis's eyes flew shut as thoughts flooded her mind. She wanted to flee and be still all at once. Images came unbidden, both sweet and shocking, of the pair of them intertwined in a way no maiden could understand.

But Ellis did understand.

The soldier's hand slid beneath the hem of her crumpled

dress, lightly caressing her leg, sweeping softly up her bare thigh.

She broke free, pushing at him. He released her, standing and stepping back from the bed. His head fell to his chest, his breathing heavy. He lifted pleading eyes to hers and leaned toward her again, but the spell was broken, the moment had passed and she took in the view of his whole face.

Ellis recoiled from the sight that met her eyes. Around his right eye there was a large blue marking in the shape of a paisley. It wandered up his forehead and into his hairline. It looked like a half mask that was starting to fade. It made everything in the sweet and terrifying moment before ugly and wrong.

She jerked backward and he snatched her hands into his again and held them fast. Her breathing was ragged as she stared.

"Am I so loathsome to you?" he asked worriedly.

"Please go!" she whispered hoarsely.

"I've come so far," he begged. "Don't send me away."

"Go!" she shouted, finally finding her voice. As she spoke, a breeze stirred the room. "Go away!"

"I brought you a present." His voice was like the keening of the wind outside. The soldier with the marred face transformed in the darkness, rapidly reducing in size and again becoming a delicate black-winged creature as the lighthouse beam searched Ellis's room. She heard a final whisper through the gale. "Widow's walk."

The French doors burst open again with a gust of the raging

storm. With a shriek the creature flew on black silky wings out of the French doors and was whisked at once into the fury of the storm.

The lighthouse beam flashed again into her room and she fell to the floor before its brilliance.

"Ellis, are you awake?" Jenny's voice pierced Ellis's thoughts.

"Jenny?" Ellis groggily clawed her way back onto the bed, exhausted. The terror of a moment before washed away as tears trickled unbidden down her cheeks.

"I heard you yelling. What's the matter?"

"Turn up the lamp, please," Ellis said weakly as she smoothed the covers. Ellis's muscles ached as though she'd been doing hard work. She glanced at the French doors, which were open, and the sheers were soaked through and flapping in the driving rain.

"Didn't I shut those doors?" Ellis asked.

"It seems not." Jenny adjusted the gaslight next to the door. Both the girls squinted in the sudden brightness as the flame flared to life.

Jenny crossed to the French doors and closed them, pushing home the bolts into the top of the frame and the matching set into the floor below. "With the curtains open doesn't the lighthouse light keep you awake?"

The statement in its ordinariness comforted Ellis and brought reality closer.

Ellis felt relief flood her body as the familiarity of sur-

roundings washed over her. The dresser with its crocheted
runner, the closet with the door slightly ajar, her mirror, the
armoire, the washstand with its china pitcher and basin were
all just as they should be. She let a sigh escape her lips and
turned to Jenny.

"You fell asleep in your new dress? It'll have to be ironed,"
Jenny pointed out as she took in Ellis's disheveled form.

"Someone was here."

Jenny's hand flew to her throat. "Who?"

A few moments before it had all seemed so real. Now,
with the light filling the room, Ellis doubted it. A sick feeling
stole over her. *Is this part of my illness?* It felt like more than a
dream and yet it was too strange to be anything else. She
paused and chose her words more carefully.

"It just seemed so real." It felt like a lie in her mouth, but
she did not know if it was.

"A dream! Oh, please tell me about it!"

"I don't know where to start . . . with the moths, I guess.
Well, they weren't really moths. . . ." She wiped the tears
away quickly as Jenny stepped forward to dab at them.

Jenny tilted up Ellis's chin. "Are you really awake, Ellie?
You're not making any sense yet."

"Well, sometimes dreams don't, you know." She smoothed
the front of her dress, trying to decide how to continue. As
she sat in the light the strangeness of the night receded.

"Today was too much. The doctor was right. I'm taking
you to see him immediately. You are obviously distressed,
unwell." Jenny looked over Ellis with some concern.

"No, don't be silly. It *had* to be a dream." Ellis straightened up and wiped her final tears away. "I'll be fine in a minute or two."

"Maybe you'll feel better if you tell me your dream," Jenny prodded.

Ellis didn't want to share with anyone what she'd experienced. The daytime restraints of her rumpled dress felt itchy and tight in this late hour of the night. She decided to change into her nightdress. She was grateful to be busy and not to have to look Jenny in the eye as she spoke. She stood and busied herself finding her nightgown.

"Well, there were all these black moths making patterns against the sheer curtain panels. And then they rushed into the room. They were all around me. There were so many I felt like I couldn't breathe and then I swallowed one."

"You swallowed a moth?" Jenny asked, a look of revulsion on her features.

A wave of nausea covered Ellis again. "It made me feel so sick. I don't want to talk about it anymore."

"Was there more?"

Ellis shrugged her shoulders, trying to sound nonchalant. "One stayed when the others left. It got bigger and became a man."

Ellis noted that Jenny's eyes lit up at the mention of "a man" and thought that she was too interested in boys and men altogether.

"Go on!" Jenny's voice warmed with interest.

"Well, I guess he was a soldier."

"A soldier? How dull. Go on, please."

"He knelt by my bedside and begged to be my suitor. He had very warm hands—"

"He touched you?"

Ellis swallowed hard. She hesitated to tell Jenny all the details of her dream, uncertain that she could explain it to herself, let alone speak of it aloud. Yet she needed to tell someone. Jenny was the only person she could trust.

"He . . ." Ellis hesitated, uncertain of the words. "He put his hand under my dress . . . slid his hands up my thigh. Oh, Jenny, it's hard to explain, but I didn't want him to stop . . . but I couldn't let him go on! Understand?"

Jenny's eyes were the size of saucers as she nodded yes and then shook her head no. She did not really understand but was fascinated, breathless, as she spoke. "What happened then?"

"And then I saw his eyes." Ellis hung the blue dress up in the closet, slipped on her nightgown and sat next to Jenny on the bed.

"What color were they?" asked Jenny.

Ellis stared at her for a moment as though she had asked about the color of creation. She answered, "Green, I guess, or maybe gray. But it wasn't the color of his eyes so much as what was behind them."

"What?" Jenny breathed excitedly.

"I thought I'd fall into his eyes and tumble into another world. Remember things."

"Did you remember something?"

"I don't know." It wasn't exactly a lie. She really didn't know what she'd felt or known or truly remembered and wanted time to ponder it alone.

"And then?"

"I sent him away," she said flatly.

"Why did you do that?" asked Jenny in complaint.

"How should I know? It was a dream—a nightmare, really."

Jenny gazed piercingly at Ellis. She shook her cropped curls from beneath her nightcap. "Was that all of it?"

"Oh, all right," said Ellis, "I'll tell you a little more, but don't laugh at me."

Jenny's expression brightened. "What?" she said.

"His face was blue."

"Blue?" echoed Jenny, a smile playing about the edges of her mouth.

"Well, not his whole face," said Ellis, trying to make it somehow seem reasonable. "It was a paisley mark around one of his eyes—like a bruise."

Jenny was smiling broadly at Ellis, who could no longer keep a straight face. They smiled at each other and a short laugh escaped their lips. Relief washed over Ellis.

Jenny said in a teasing tone that mocked the doctor, "My dear, you sent him away because of a blue paisley? My, you've gotten finicky about your suitors!"

"Oh, stop it!" begged Ellis. "You promised not to laugh." She tried to feign a pout, but it was no use; her smile ruined it.

"Feel better?" asked Jenny.

"Yes, thank you." Ellis leaned back against the headboard and sighed. The two girls looked at each other and Ellis felt a giggle rising in her throat, which she forcibly swallowed.

"We'd better put out the light and stop laughing or I'll never get any real rest tonight," she said.

"You? What about me?" complained Jenny. "I shall be concerned all night that you were haunted by a paisley suitor or was it a paisley suit?" Jenny stifled a giggle.

Ellis jumped up and tiptoed across the cold floor to the closet. "Perhaps it was a paisley suit after all," she said facetiously. "In which case, I'll shut the closet door so I'll have no more bad dreams tonight. Jen, please turn down the gas and draw the heavy curtains, will you? I don't want moths gathering at the windows. I'd never sleep."

Jenny peered through the doors. "Don't worry; there are only itty-bitty white ones out there, Ellie. I will protect you, m'lady." Jenny struck a gallant pose as though wielding a sword and then bowed. Ellis rolled her eyes but secretly appreciated the gesture. She began to feel drowsy. The terror was past.

Jenny gently turned the gas lamp key and the room was bathed in moonlight again for a moment before she pulled the drapes shut. "You know, Ellie, nightbird is just another name for 'moth.' Maybe that's where your dream came from," she said thoughtfully before she left the room and shut the door.

I wish I knew where anything about me came from, thought Ellis ruefully. She hopped nimbly into bed, her feet numb from the coldness of the floor. She did not notice the white flower petals that had fallen by the bed and now clung to her toes.

She dug deeply into the covers of her bed, relieved she had managed to avoid telling Jenny all the details of what had happened. As she closed her eyes intimate images floated into her inner vision and shocked her once again with their intensity. She forced herself to think of the afternoon she'd spent at the Nightbirds Literary Society. They had flitted about drawn to the next interesting thing like moths to a flame. She thought about dancing with Merrick and how he'd offered to shelter her and Jenny. Drained and exhausted, at last she slept.

In the moonlight silky-winged moths danced and one lone dark figure sat in the shadows of the garden below keeping close watch over Ellis's little balcony.

11

CANVAS AND PAINT

Despite the frightful storm, Ellis awakened filled with energy and hope. The bright morning streaming in between the heavy drapes stripped away the strangeness she'd felt in the night. She rose from the bed, crossing to the French doors. Unknown possibilities in the day spread their arms wide to her as she pulled back the velvet curtains, opened the doors and gazed onto the pristine morning over the harbor toward the lighthouse. Towering white clouds patched with bright blue were all that remained of the tempest. She leaned against the doorway. The tang of salt mingled with the scent of the roses below as she filled her lungs with morning air.

She noted the narrow stairs off her balcony leading up to the widow's walk. *Widow's walk,* she thought ruefully. It was the last thing she had heard in her nightmare. She squared her shoulders and shook off thoughts of the strange suitor, his touch and the blue mark on his face.

"Widow's walk indeed," she muttered to herself, then shook her head in chagrin at her own nonsensical dreams.

The view from her balcony was lovely, but it was eclipsed by the roof of the house and she wondered what it was like up by the cupola. She hesitated at the bottom step for just a moment and then ran to the top as though racing against her own will. She refused to allow one vivid nightmare to haunt her in the daylight.

At the top of the stairs she found the narrow walkway that surrounded the circular glassed-in cupola. She followed the railing around the widow's walk toward the water, taking in the view. From this vantage point she could see not only the lighthouse island but the entire sweep of the harbor and across to the town. Boats bobbed in the water and their pilots barked rough greetings to each other. She shaded her eyes and gazed across the bay and saw smoke curl toward the sky from chimneys. The little town of Gamin buzzed with morning activity. She felt the tendrils of the sun's rays warm her back. She turned around and noted that past the cupola she could see the glimmer of open sea outside the bay on her left. Turning back, she stole a glance at the lighthouse and thought she saw movement, but the figures were indistinct in the distance. She wished she had the spyglass she'd left downstairs on the porch.

It was a lovely scene, but she didn't feel a part of it. She felt as though she'd been on vacation for too long and longed to be home. *I need something to do,* she thought.

She retraced her steps around the widow's walk and paused at the top of the stairs when she saw something inside the cupola that caught her eye. She went to the glass door of the cupola and opened it. It was quite dusty inside, much like her room had been when she arrived. Large cushions lay scattered on generously wide counterpanes at the base of the surrounding windows that invited her to be seated. But to sit was not the reason she had entered. In the center of the room there stood what she had glimpsed from the stairs: an artist's easel.

At the foot of the easel was a stack of small to large blank sheets of paper. She picked up one of the heavy, ragged-edged papers and ran her fingers over it. It had a rough tooth to it.

Watercolor paper. The certainty of the thought sent a thrill up her spine. *Dancing, yes, because I proved it yesterday, and maybe the piano, too, but beyond a doubt I know I can do this.* The ghost of a memory stole over her fingers and she could sense how the weight of a small paintbrush felt in her hand.

She turned on her heel, her eyes searching the room until she spied what she knew must be there: a wooden case. It peeked from its hiding place beneath a large cushion on the window seat to her right.

Ignoring the dusty floor, she knelt next to the seat and tugged the case by its leather handles, sliding it from beneath the cushion. She turned the clasp and opening it found a treasure of small tubes that were printed with the words "Moist Colour." There was an assortment of brushes, a pencil, a white cotton rag and a small, round tin about the same size as a lady's powder compact. To Ellis's delight, the tin contained a dozen small, square cakes of dry paint. She knew this item was meant to be carried in a pocket in case one happened on a scene insisting to be recorded.

She had found a task she was eager to try. She could see as

she inspected the case's contents that it had been used. She paused and looked about her. *These must be Jenny's things. I'll ask to use them,* she thought. She picked up the little compact and slipped it into her pocket. As she stood up she spied a handle on the floor next to the wall to one side of the door. She bent down and tugged. A small, square trapdoor opened up in the floor. She could see stairs leading down into the darkness. Where the steps descended to she couldn't imagine. She shut the odd little hatch, making a mental note to ask Jenny about it later. She tidied the room and closed the door behind her.

She patted the little tin in her pocket and smiled.

"It is absolutely the most dreadful thing ever to happen here in Gamin!"

Martha's voice floated up the curving stairs as Ellis descended toward the rotunda and the parlor beyond. Ellis recognized Martha's voice from the luncheon of the day before but was surprised, since her giggling, excited tones hardly seemed congruous with the statement.

"Shocking, if you ask me," Alicia was saying, "which, of course, is why Martha insisted we had to come and tell you all the details at once."

"Shocking, Alicia?" Jenny, Alicia and Martha were bent together in quiet conversation that was eclipsed by Ellis's entrance.

"Good morning, Ellie," said Martha. She giggled a bit and Alicia nudged her in the ribs. "Difficult night?"

Ellis blushed. "Whatever do you mean?"

"Jenny says you've been dreaming." Alicia gave her a quizzical look as though questioning the possibility of such a thing.

"About a moth boyfriend." Despite Alicia's tug on her arm, Martha's smile crept into place. "It sounds . . . wonderful."

Ellis stopped short of joining the group and looked at Jenny. *How could you?* she wondered.

Jenny looked at the carpet instead of at Ellis. It was a small betrayal, but it was there in the room between them and made Ellis wish she had stayed in the cupola.

Ellis swallowed the angry words on her tongue and instead managed to casually say, "Well, I guess everyone has crazy dreams."

"Of course we all do sometimes," Jenny agreed, looking up gratefully at Ellis.

"Jenny says you cried out in your sleep . . . that you dreamed about moths and a hideous suitor." Alicia asked sharply, "What was all that about?"

Ellis didn't like or understand Alicia's tone. Ellis's shoulders tensed. Talking about the dream was bringing back the feeling of terror she'd had in the dark. Ellis shook her head and shrugged her aching shoulders. "It was only a dream. It wasn't *about* anything."

The group in front of her seemed hungry, but for what she didn't know and a feeling of guardedness stole over her. She had the uncanny feeling that if she bolted from the room and back up the stairs they would chase her like a pack of hounds. She licked her lips, took a step back and searched for a new subject of conversation.

"It seems to me you were about to tell us your own shocking news," Ellis said beneath arched eyebrows.

"Oh, indeed we are!" Martha spoke in breathy excitement as she bit her lip and smiled. "It's shocking *and* terrible!"

"Martha, please," Alicia huffed in exasperation. "The word is all over town and we thought it best to bring it to you ourselves. There's been a death in Gamin. A young woman has been killed."

"Oh, not just *killed*." Martha nearly bounced with the news. "Torn asunder so badly, by all accounts, that they have not actually recovered the body. Just a foot, I believe . . . although according to Ely Rossini her blood and gore fairly painted the rocks on Dillingham Point—"

"Martha, really!" Alicia snapped.

"Well, that's what Ely said," Martha sniffed. "Dr. Carmichael told him he didn't know what to make of the stench or the discoloration of the woman's skin. He said that he had never experienced such a thing before. He found it most illuminating."

"Putrification on that scale meant that she must have been dead for some time, certainly at least a week," Ellis said thoughtfully.

Jenny and Alicia looked aghast at Ellis.

"Really?" Martha asked in surprise.

Ellis blinked. "I . . . I'm sorry; I don't know why I said that! I just can't believe it. A woman . . . murdered here in Gamin?"

"Yes, that is what we came out to tell you," Alicia said impatiently, as though Ellis had not been paying attention. "Fortunately, they found her remains before the storm last night or most of the signs might have been washed away. They may never have discovered her death."

"Was she . . . was she anyone we know?" Jenny asked.

"No, I believe the young woman was an outsider," Alicia said. "A painter by all accounts. She was working on a painting of Curtis Lighthouse out on the point. The constable has yet to find her art box or paints. He believes that whoever committed the crime must have taken them with them."

"A painter?" Ellis asked. "How very odd. . . ."

"What is it, Ellis?" Jenny asked.

"It's strange, isn't it?" Ellis mused aloud. "I saw a young woman—with dark hair, as I recall—carrying an easel through the train station just yesterday. So it couldn't have been the victim. I almost felt like I knew her. But I don't really know anybody anymore, do I?"

Her hand found the paint tin in her pocket.

"What a coincidence!" She held out the little compact and showed it to the group. "I found this and an easel and other art supplies scattered about up in the cupola. I assume they're yours, Jenny?"

Jenny took it from Ellis's hand and turned it over to examine it. "No, I don't think so. I never did much painting, except a little one in the workroom. I wonder how long it's been up there?"

"Don't, Jenny." Alicia stepped forward, grabbing the compact and shoving it back into Ellis's hands. "I suspect the constable needs to hear about this."

"Constable?" Jenny swallowed and stood very still. "Does Merrick know?"

"I don't know. He should. How could he not know?" Alicia bit the words off roughly.

Ellis stood there, lips apart, her brow furrowed, trying to comprehend their conversation. Finally becoming impatient, she asked, "Why is it so impossible that terrible things could happen here? There's a war raging in France . . . why should Gamin be exempt?"

"You." Alicia stepped close and spoke the words inches from Ellis's face. "It's you. You've brought this here."

Martha groaned.

Coming to Ellis's defense, Jenny took Alicia's arm and pulled her a step back. "Alicia! Don't be ridiculous. Ellis has come here because she's been ill. Just like I was. We should be kind to her."

"Yes, just like you." Alicia yanked Jenny's hand off her arm and continued speaking to Ellis. "Where did the art supplies come from? If they aren't Jenny's, whose are they? You know more about all this than you're saying, don't you?"

Ellis's mouth went dry and her cheeks grew warm as the barrage of Alicia's words hit her. She shoved the little tin of paints deep into her pocket. *She can't think I have something to do with this artist's murder?*

"I might not remember much," Ellis's words tumbled out, "but I know that I have no connection whatsoever to the horrible things you're talking about. And as far as the paints and canvasses from the cupola go, everything was a dusty mess up there when I discovered them, as though no one had been there for years. And besides, this woman they found has to have been dead for at least a week."

"Ellis wasn't here a week ago," Martha's mild voice cut across Ellis's words.

"That's right!" Jenny turned to Alicia.

Alicia's face fell. She opened her mouth and closed it again. Ellis thought she saw disappointment cross the other girl's face. An apology from Alicia for her crazy insinuations didn't seem forthcoming.

Ellis studied the carpet. *Is she hoping that I'm some sort of monster? I don't understand. Does Alicia know something about me that I don't? The artist died before I arrived. Arrived from where, though? Why am I here? Why can't I just go home?* Her throat constricted as her thoughts spun in the vacuum of her life and she looked up to find three pairs of eyes all silently watching her.

Alicia, however, would not be so easily deterred. "When the constable finds out about those paints and canvasses—"

"I suspect," came the smooth voice from the rotunda, "he will be as appreciative of Ellis's talents as I am."

The three women were startled.

"Forgive us for letting ourselves in," Merrick said with a crooked smile. Two young men stood behind him. "We've come to offer you a diversion."

12

PLAY

*M*artha gave a nervous giggle. Alicia turned away, a sudden flush coming to her cheeks. Ellis stood aghast that the men had entered Summersend unbidden and unannounced.

It was Jenny who broke the awkward moment, rushing up to the tall, older man with gushing exuberance. "Oh, Merrick, how very good of you to come! We're in need of some diversion . . . our conversations have turned entirely too serious."

"Indeed, have they?" Merrick asked, though his eyes were fixed on Ellis. He brushed past Jenny without a glance. He stood too close to Ellis, his sad, haunting eyes looking down on her. "And what topic so fascinates our ladies today?"

"Oh, well!" Martha purred. "Ellis had a dream!"

Ellis blushed, trying to catch the other woman's eye.

"A dream?" Merrick spoke to Martha, but he still looked

on Ellis with a cool, unblinking gaze. "How extraordinary. What kind of dream?"

Martha saw the pleading look but plunged on anyway. "A nightmare, I believe. She was in her nightdress and a man came into her room during the storm, touching her in a way that—"

"Martha!" Ellis snapped. "Hold your tongue!"

The young woman stopped speaking, a look of hurt and confusion coming over her face.

"It's quite all right, Ellis. Miss Kendrick means well." Merrick chuckled in his deep voice. He inclined his head toward Alicia. "And what of you, Miss Van der Meer? I trust that now you are also thoroughly apprised of our Ellis's shocking dreams?"

Ellis blinked in disbelief. Did Merrick really mean for them to discuss her intimate dreams in the parlor?

"Yes, Mr. Bacchus," Alicia said, still not looking the man in the eye. "I believe I am thoroughly acquainted with Miss Harkington's sordid imaginings."

"We were discussing the young woman's murder," Ellis interjected. She was mortified and desperate to change the topic of conversation.

"Rather strange business, that," said the young man with the brown curly hair and the slightly bug-eyed look standing behind Merrick. Ellis recognized him as Ely from the previous day. "I'm sorry that you ladies have to have been troubled about it."

"You are, of course, acquainted with Mr. Ely Rossini."

Merrick's chin raised slightly, his head nodding slightly in the direction of the young men. "Joining us is Mr. Silenus Tune."

"Pleasure, ma'am," Silenus said as he nodded in the direction of Ellis. He was slightly shorter than Ely, with a young, clean-shaven look. Ellis thought he had the kind of face that would look perpetually younger than his years would allow. There was a mischievous one-sided cant to his smile that left Ellis feeling wary.

Ellis nodded slightly toward the young men.

"Miss Van der Meer," Merrick said, turning toward Alicia, "I should not trouble the constable about Ellis's hobbies. He is far too occupied at the moment with idle gossip. I would much prefer that you visit me later in the day and express what you have observed to me at that time. Permit me to determine whether your thoughts have any merits which warrant troubling our constable."

"Of course, Mr. Bacchus," Alicia started. "But I no longer think that is necessary—"

"Of course you must," Merrick chided. "It is your duty."

Alicia swallowed. "I really should not take up your time—"

"But I insist," Merrick said. There was menace in his smile.

"It would be my pleasure," Alicia said, looking away from Merrick once again.

"That being settled, we have come to invite you all on an outing," Merrick said, turning his most charming smile back on Ellis. "The storm has driven a ship up on the East Shore not far from here. I propose that we avail ourselves of this novelty today."

Martha clapped in excited approval.

Alicia, Ely and Silenus all smiled at one another in anticipation.

"Oh, how delightful," Jenny said, entwining her arm around Merrick's.

"You cannot be serious," Ellis sputtered.

The other young people looked at her in disbelief.

Merrick inclined his head, his eyes fixed on her. "Why, Ellis, you're spoiling the fun."

"What of its crew and passengers?" Ellis demanded. "Has anything been done for their safety or their recovery? Who is caring for the injured?"

"You need not concern yourself with the passengers or the crew," Merrick said in soothing tones, his perfect teeth beaming with his warmest smile. "They are no longer aboard."

"Then we can hardly go traipsing about someone's property," Ellis continued. "The owner of the ship—"

"Would be my uncle in Portland," Merrick interrupted. "He has authorized me to take charge of the vessel, her cargo and the passengers' personal effects. So, you see, it is all quite proper, Ellis."

She stared back at him. "That sounds rather a bit too convenient, Mr. Bacchus."

"Quite the contrary," Merrick replied with a studied and cool, gracious manner. "If I tell you something about Gamin, you of all people may rest assured that it is already, absolutely true."

.   .   .

The party left the porch of Summersend and proceeded down the lane on foot. Merrick had offered Ellis his arm and she had taken it perfunctorily and come at once to regret it. He had clapped his left hand over hers, pinning her to his arm like one of Jenny's moths in the bell jar, pulling her with him as he strode down the muddy dirt road.

Jenny followed somewhat sullenly after them as Alicia, Martha, Ely and Silenus chattered around her, excited for the promised diversion to come. All of the women's hems were stained almost at once by the muddy pools of dirty water that remained from the previous night's terrible storm, but the women seemed to take no notice of the state of their clothing, the ruining of the cloth or their mud-caked shoes.

"A wrecked ship!" Martha exclaimed. "We must go and see it! We must!"

"It's just down at the harbor. . . ."

The voice came unbidden from somewhere deep in Ellis's memory, chilling her so quickly that she shivered in the morning sun. It was a young voice, devoid of any connection in time or context.

"Everyone is going! Hurry!"

Dread flooded through Ellis. She felt her face go pale, a cold perspiration breaking on her brow.

"Please, Mr. Bacchus, I'm n-n-not well," she stammered. "I must return to the house."

"It's just your nerves, Ellis. I won't have it." Merrick

pressed his hand down on hers with a strength that made her wince. "Besides, we're already here."

Olive cloth. Clear glass. Red light.

"Come look! It's just at the harbor's edge. You can see it through the window! Isn't it thrilling?" Her smile was so excited just before she died. . . .

Ellis cried out.

Merrick ignored her distress and pulled Ellis through the trees above the seawall and onto the beach, the rest of the group rushing out onto the sands after them, chattering with excitement. The crashing of the waves was still carrying some of the force from the storm that had passed, breaking loudly along the shoreline.

The *Mary Celeste* lay high up on the shore, her hull broken on the near side against a rock outcropping that rose up from sands. The sails were torn and shredded, flapping uselessly in the offshore breeze. A rope ladder lay over the near side of the ship, falling down over the rocks on which the hull was leaning.

"Oh, do you suppose the people are still on the ship?" Martha asked in breathless excitement.

"They might be," Silenus teased. "Maybe they're dead!"

"Really, Sil, you mustn't get her hopes up." Alicia laughed.

"Oh, how thrilling!" Martha tittered.

"Isn't it thrilling?" The girls' voices echoed in Ellis's mind. Fuzzy images pressed in against the edges of her inner vision.

"I . . . I can't," Ellis balked.

"Oh, of course you can," Merrick said, pulling her toward the grounded ship. "We all can."

"No, I beg you to allow me to return to the house." Ellis's breath was quick and shallow, her words shaking as she spoke them. "I . . . I don't think the doctor would approve."

"But he has," Merrick assured her. He pulled her up onto the rock outcropping. "He and I discussed it just this morning. What are you afraid of, Ellis?"

"This ship . . . there's something familiar about—"

"Oh, Ellis, must you stand in everyone's way?" Jenny groused.

"Quite so," Merrick said. He swung his leg up onto the deck, then reached back, gripping Ellis this time not by the hand but firmly around her wrist. With remarkable strength he pulled her up from the rocks and onto the deck of the ship. "But it would be far worse to stand in your own way. This is just the sort of thing you used to love."

The deck of the ship leaned at strange angles, slanting backward toward where the cabins were located and slightly to one side. Ellis gripped the rail of the ship with white, bloodless hands. Silenus followed her aboard almost at once and began pulling the other women in their party aboard. In moments, Alicia, Jenny and Martha were joined by Ely and Silenus as they ranged back along the broken deck, prattling constantly with one another as they pointed out the most mundane of the broken ship's pieces with the greatest of curiosity.

Ellis drew in a shuddering breath.

"All these terrors you fear are just ghosts of your own imaginings. You shiver in the darkness, you cry out in the night and then the lamps are lit and the sun comes up and all your fears are found to be shadows—dispelled once someone just shines a little light on them." Merrick left her to explore the back of the ship. "I disagree with the doctor on one point: I do not think you need to remember your past at all. It was a bad dream and better left behind. Come back to us, Ellis, and leave your unpleasant dreams behind."

Ellis stayed by the railing, thinking about what Merrick had said. The ship had brought memories up from her past, but what if it was a past she really wanted to forget? What if something so terrible had happened to her that her mind refused to let her remember it? Wouldn't it be better to let such memories remain buried?

She thought of the dream she had of the man in her room the night before. It was, she reminded herself, only a dream, a fantasy woven out of her own imaginings. Maybe Merrick's counsel was right; perhaps she did need to leave her unpleasant dreams behind.

"A play! A play!" Silenus burst from the doorway leading to the aft cabins dragging something heavy behind him. "We must have a play!"

"Oh yes!" Martha exclaimed.

"What is that?" Alicia asked, trying to peer around Silenus.

The young man swung the bulky object scraping across the deck planks to rest in front of him.

It was a large steamer chest. A number of shipping labels stood affixed to its leather exterior, as well as several identification tags.

"I found it inside," the young man replied. "There are more in the cabins . . . surely enough for everyone!"

Martha clapped her hands merrily and hurried toward the aft doorway. Alicia followed her almost at once, pulling down her parasol and laying it against a rack of belaying pins on the far rail. Jenny smiled and hurried to join them. Ely shrugged and followed, although with notable reluctance.

"Mr. Bacchus!" Ellis said. Her outrage drove her from the rail toward the patron. "You must put a stop to this!"

"Whatever do you mean?" Merrick asked, looking down at her.

Silenus flipped open the dual latches, raising the lid. He pulled out a jacket and an embroidered shawl, smiled and then wrapped himself in both.

"These are someone's private possessions!" Ellis said.

"Yes," Merrick agreed. "And as I do not see anyone present to lay claim to them, at this moment they are *my* private possessions to do with as I please. And I think a play sounds most pleasing indeed."

Alicia emerged from the cabin door wearing a plain print dress and an apron. Dark, foul stains ran down one side of the dress around a long tear in the fabric. She was followed at once by Martha in an ill-fitting silk dress with a wide skirt. It, too, was stained from the neckline down to the waist. She held a doll dangling by one foot at her side. Jenny emerged a moment later in a black mourning dress and a lace cap. Last came Ely, wearing a captain's peacoat and cap with a pipe in his hand.

"Most excellent," Merrick proclaimed. "What shall be your play, Mr. Tune?"

"Oh, I should think 'The Tragic End of the *Mary Celeste.*'" Silenus grinned. "Alicia, how do you die?"

"I shall be murdered by my husband who was driven mad during the storm," Alicia proclaimed as she clasped her hands to her chest. "I haven't decided quite yet how, but I'm sure it will come to me."

"Oh, and me, too," Jenny enthused, waving her crippled hand in the hopes of being acknowledged. "I caught him in the act and he murdered me, too!"

"Oh, that is good." Merrick smiled.

Jenny beamed at his attentions.

"Well, I suppose that makes me the murderous husband," Silenus acknowledged with his own bow. "I'll have to have killed the crew, as well, I suppose."

"Except for me," Ely said.

"Why except for you?" Silenus demanded. "Why should you be different?"

"Because I'm the one who drove you into the storm," Ely affirmed. "I had hopes of killing you in the storm before you killed me."

Silenus frowned. "But I was driven mad *by* the storm."

"And what about me?" Martha demanded, stamping her foot. The doll twisted, barely noticed in her grip.

"You are why I drove the ship into the storm," Ely proclaimed. "You can be my wife and you were going to run away from me with Silenus."

"But what do I do with *this*?" Martha asked.

She held the doll up in front of her, dangling from the single foot by which she gripped it, its face turned away from Ellis.

"Where did you get that?" Ellis demanded.

"It was just sitting on the bunk in one of the cabins," Martha said. "It didn't belong to anyone."

"There was a *child* on board?" Ellis was aghast. "Give it to me!"

"It's broken," Martha said, holding out the doll. "I didn't think you wanted to play."

Ellis snatched the doll from Martha's grasp and turned it over.

"No!" Ellis breathed in horror.

Everyone stopped at once, staring at her.

The doll's porcelain face was broken. A curved section of her forehead was missing, dropping down over where her right eye had been.

Ellis screamed, dropping the doll on the deck. The porcelain head shattered against the planking. She knelt on the rough wood of the deck and, choking back tears she didn't understand, began gingerly picking up the china shards.

The party froze as all eyes turned upon Ellis.

"Ellie, stop. It's not worth fixing." Merrick's hand was firmly under her elbow, pulling her up.

"But some little child will be so heartbroken." Ellis gestured to the broken doll.

"A child?"

"Yes, like the little boy at the lighthouse." Ellis heard the gasps of those about her.

Merrick's grip bit sharply into the flesh of her arm. "That's not possible," he told her in low tones.

"Whatever can you mean?" She looked up and saw on his face concern warring with irritation.

"Disgusting," spat Alicia. Martha, next to her, shivered and looked away.

"I don't understand. Did something happen to the children? Where are they?" Ellis's features tightened into a ball of perplexity as Merrick held her gaze. "Please, please help me," she begged.

Merrick drew himself up as if to answer, but Silenus stepped between Ellis and Merrick, causing Merrick to release his grip on Ellis's arm. "It's quite simple, really. There are no children in Gamin. Never have been. Never will be. Guess we're as close as it gets. It's for the best, you see."

But Ellis did not see. She spun on her heel till her gaze fell on Jenny, who silently shook her head in agreement. Ellis realized the only child she'd seen since her arrival was the boy at the lighthouse and now had been told that even that was impossible.

She desperately wanted to tell Silenus, Merrick and all of them that they were mad but held her tongue, knowing that she was the one who'd been brought here to get well. She swallowed and once again found herself desperate for air, for escape.

Ellis fled to the rail and down the ladder, desperate to get away from the doll, from the ship and the voices that spoke to her as she ran across the sands and back toward Summersend.

As she blindly stumbled forward the image of a young woman floated up from her memory. "It's just down at the harbor. . . . Come, see!"

And the girl smiled the moment before she died. . . .

· · ·

Jenny's bell jar of pinned moths stood on a small table near the entrance to Summersend. Ellis paused as she noted that Jenny had added more to her collection. The specimens were becoming quite crowded, though Jenny would never admit to adding any. Ellis thought she saw the wings of the great luna moth inside twitch.

It was too much. Ellis lunged toward the stairs, grabbed the railing and ran up the steps two at a time.

The sound of the ocean against the shore and a lazy pool of sunlight greeted her as she crossed the threshold of her room.

Sanctuary.

She shook uncontrollably, weeping. It must have all been a dream—*had* to have been a dream. The man in her room with the paisley mark over his face, the terrible thrill of his touch, they were both things of her imagination. She could not have seen the artist in the train station—she had died at least a week before. It all had to be in Ellis's dreams.

She looked about her, fighting to control her breathing.

The room was real. The French doors were real. The trunk and the closet were both real. The dresser, the vanity, the bed . . . *The bed is real. I saw the girl die. There are no children here. Are these real?* She needed to touch the solid furniture pieces, to reassure herself that something was real and that she could tell the difference between her waking days and her nightmares.

She kicked off her shoes and crossed toward the bed, tears already blurring her vision.

As she stepped next to the bed, something sharp bit into her foot through her stockings.

Gasping at the sharp little shock of pain, she picked up her foot and found a thorny limp white rose clinging to it. She reached down with a shaky hand and pulled out three thorns from the bottom of her foot through her stocking. A droplet of blood spread in a small circle on the bottom of her snagged stocking.

Ellis began to scream.

13

THE MANOR

An unseasonably cold wind spun the leaves in a small cyclone around the two women huddled together against the squall gathering in the late afternoon over Penobscot Bay. The previously clear skies had darkened with the onset of the thunderstorm rolling in from the sea. Lightning was already lancing across the sky as the pair approached the towering façade of the Norembega mansion. The stonework of its walls was bathed in a deepening red of a sunset retreating before the second storm while the black of its curved and clapboard woodwork seemed almost silhouetted against the fury approaching from beyond its massive shape.

"Jenny, please," Ellis said over the wind. "We shouldn't have come."

"I won't hear it," Jenny said in a voice that would brook no contradiction. "Look at you! Your hands won't stop shaking and you haven't been able to stop crying since I found you after returning from the shipwreck."

"I'll be all right," Ellis said, though she was, in fact, not sure at all. What she knew was that the house they were approaching filled her with a sense both of the familiar and of foreboding. "Just take me home."

"You have to see the doctor and that's all there is to it," Jenny replied, pulling her toward the gravel-paved drive and the stairs of the enclosed entry. Fitted stone pillars supported the ornate woodwork of the steeply gabled roof, the glass-filled arch of the window over the entry doors dark and staring down on them. Ellis shuddered under its gaze, but Jenny pulled her up the steps, pushing open the dull black doors with their own dark panes of glass and drawing her into its maw.

Ellis could not stop shaking. Jenny had tried to console her throughout the afternoon, but the vision of the white rose and the thorns staining her stocking with her blood surfaced again and again in her mind. It was real, but it could not be real. She tried again and again to rationalize the presence of the thorny rose in her room, thinking that perhaps someone else had put it there or that in a fit she had brought it herself and forgotten about it . . . but try as she might her mind could not accept those explanations and she was left with a horror that her mind could not resolve. Either madness was happening about her or she was mad herself . . . and both divergent realities frightened every part of her being.

Jenny reached up for the bell chain and pulled it. A distant, muted metallic trilling sounded from somewhere beyond the heavy door. They stood in the vestibule for long moments.

"Oh, bother!" Jenny did not hesitate. She gripped the latch and pushed through the heavy oak door into the house.

"Jenny! No!" Ellis begged.

The entry room beyond was dim. The sudden onset of the thunderclouds outside had prematurely darkened the interior and the lamps had not yet been lit. The ornate parquet floor and the oak wood paneling up to the wainscoting, as well as the wooden coffered ceiling overhead, made the space feel darker still. Two alcoves were set into the far corners of the room, both closed off with doors that led deeper into the house. On Ellis's left was an ornate oak staircase. A short flight of stairs there led up to a small landing featuring a caller's sitting area with its own fireplace before the stairs doubled back and rose up through the coffered ceiling to the upper reaches of the house. To Ellis's right, a large set of double doors were open to a long sitting room and, through an arched opening past a cornered fireplace, what appeared to be the rounded interior wall of a turret.

"Jenny, please," Ellis said under her breath. "I'm not well."

"Which is precisely why you need to see the doctor," Jenny affirmed.

"We haven't been invited in!" Ellis choked out the words, trying desperately not to start sobbing again.

"Merrick said we were to come and so we have," Jenny said. "I've been here many times, Ellis, and we are perfectly welcome. I don't understand why Merrick has not come to greet us. Listen, you wait here for me and I'll go find the doctor for you."

"No," Ellis breathed. "Please stay with me."

"I'll only be a moment," Jenny insisted, prying Ellis's grip off her arm. "Two shakes of a dead lamb's tail and I'll be right back with the doctor."

Jenny patted Ellis's hand and then disappeared through the left-hand door at the end of the entry hall, closing the door behind her.

Ellis drew in a long, shuddering breath. She glanced at the chairs on the landing and considered for a moment availing herself of them but somehow could not bring herself to climb up even those three short steps. She did not want to think about this place or the terrible haunting things that were drifting unbidden into her mind. The rumble of distant thunder beyond the walls made the intermediate silences all the more unbearable.

She was desperate for something to distract her.

A flash of lightning stabbed through the windows, casting the parlor into bright relief. Faces stared back at her from paintings on the wall. The stone carvings of griffins on either side of the fireplace glared menacingly at her. They all receded once more into obscurity, but in that moment she could clearly see the round-walled room beyond the parlor, its high windows set into the curve of the thick wall and something beneath them that brought a smile to the corners of her mouth.

The wall beneath the curving glass panes was lined with bookshelves.

Ellis sighed inwardly. To lose herself in the words and shutter her thoughts for a time, she thought, would be comfort indeed.

She stepped quietly into the parlor, the darkness surrounding her. It threatened to close in on her fragile mind, the faces of the dark paintings following her soft steps across the parquet floor, but she kept her eyes fixed on the bookshelves of the library beyond. Each flash of lightning startled her, but she came to accept them as her friend, showing her the way back toward the ordered sanity of the written word.

The room was a half circle, the inner wall flat while the outer wall followed the curve of the turret. As she entered she noticed a small desk around the side. An oil lamp stood next to a matchbox atop the short bookshelves as they curved beneath the windows. She pulled the glass from the top of the lamp, struck the match on the box and lit the wick. Quickly replacing the glass, she trimmed the lamp and turned with anticipation to the books on the shelves.

She blinked for a moment, uncertain at what she was seeing. She took up the lamp and moved it closer to the books on the shelves.

Though the shelves were filled with many volumes of different sizes and bindings, none of them carried any lettering on their spines. No titles, no authors, no identity of any kind.

Ellis frowned. She reached out with her free hand, pulling a random volume from off the shelf. She set the lamp back down atop the bookshelf and took the book in both hands.

The cover did not budge. Ellis's brow furrowed and she turned the book over in her hands.

Wood. The book was a fake . . . a piece of wood carved into the likeness of a bound tome.

Ellis pulled several more of the books from the shelf.

Each one was a replica made of carved wood.

Ellis set each of the books back in its place and straightened up. She believed that seeing a person's library could tell you a great deal about who that person was inside.

"It would seem," Ellis muttered to herself, "that our Mr. Merrick is nothing at all."

She took up the lamp again from off the top of the shelves. *What is taking Jenny so long?* Ellis was about to return to the entry hall and at least step back into the vestibule when something on the little desk caught her eye.

A book, a real book.

Ellis stepped over to the desk to take a closer look at it. The cover was a pale green with gold embossing in an elegant script. The title shone in her lamplight.

Gamin.

"A history, perhaps," Ellis muttered as she set down the lamp on the desk this time and picked up the book. "I wonder if there is anything in here about me."

She started to open the book.

"What are you doing!" came the sharp, demanding voice behind her.

Ellis started, dropping the book with a loud thud back onto the desktop.

"Oh, Mr. Bacchus, I—"

"What are you doing in my home?" Merrick stepped uncomfortably close to her. "Who invited you to paw through my personal effects?"

She backed up against the desk as he stared intensely down at her. The legs of the writing table scraped against the wood floor as it shifted. "No one! That is, Jenny brought me here. She is the one who insisted—"

"Jenny! I might have known," Merrick grumbled. "Where is she?"

"I d-d-don't know," Ellis stammered. "She left me here to find Dr. Carmichael."

Merrick took a step back, the lines in his face softening. He wore trousers but was barefoot. Ellis blushed slightly; the man was wearing no shirt under his robe, which he had cinched closed at the waist. He fingered an ornate silver key that flashed as he turned it in his hand. "Of course, Ellis; she is only concerned for you, as are all of us. You gave us quite a fright out at the shipwreck earlier today. As you are here seeking the doctor, I suspect you are not feeling much improved?"

"Jenny worries perhaps a bit too much," Ellis said.

"Well, in any event she'll not find the doctor here." Merrick reached for the lantern on the desk. Picking it up, he moved back toward the sitting room. Ellis, not wishing to be left behind in the darkening room, followed him. "The doctor seems to have tired of my company. He has taken up lodgings in Hobson's Inn just down High Street. It's not far from here. I can have him brought here if necessary."

"No, I'm sure we can manage." Ellis sat carefully down on a beautifully upholstered couch between the two windows on the west side of the room. Her eyes were becoming accustomed to the light from the lamp. The warm tones illuminating the sitting room and gently banishing the deeper shadows across the faces of the wall portraits. "I wish Jenny would return. I cannot imagine what is keeping her."

"The Norembega is a bit labyrinthine, Ellis. A silly girl like Jenny could easily lose her way and find it difficult to get back to where she began." Merrick set the lamp on the mantel over the cornered fireplace. The library now was entirely cast in shadow. Despite the various gas lamps fixed to the walls about the room, Merrick made no move to light them. "Still, the layout of the house is not unknown to her; I have every confidence that she will find her way back to you . . . as you have found your way back to us."

"We tried the bell, sir," Ellis explained. "But no one answered."

"I was in the carriage house tending to a few things." Merrick turned toward the mantel, dropping the silver key into a cut-glass bowl that rested there. "Nothing important . . . just making sure everything was secure from the storm. I've only just returned to the house."

"It appears to be a most interesting home," Ellis said as she glanced about the room. She desperately wanted to turn the conversation away from herself. "You keep it immaculately well. The floors are so perfectly polished and without a speck of dust. It is quite impressive, sir."

"You approve of it, then?" Merrick asked with a smile.

"Why, yes, I suppose I do," Ellis lied. There was something about the home that both drew her and made her distrustful at the same time, like a woman who was too perfect in her appearance. Still, it seemed to Ellis that Merrick Bacchus took considerable pride in his home. "Perhaps you might show me the Norembega of yours on some future visit. I should be glad to take a turn about the grounds and outbuildings as well as the house itself when—"

"My property is not to be the subject of idle curiosity," Merrick said, his manner suddenly cold and harsh once more. "As to the grounds, you may look where you like, but stay clear of the carriage house, Ellis. It is dangerous and certainly no place for any young woman."

"Why would I want to go into—"

"Stay out of the carriage house, Ellis!" Merrick repeated, his voice a low growl. "It is absolutely forbidden!"

"I understand." Ellis blinked, pulling her wrap closer around her shoulders.

"Do you understand, Ellis?" Merrick asked, stepping closer to where she sat. She tensed up at his approach. "What do you *really* understand?"

He reached down, taking her hands and drawing her up off the couch. His grip was so painful that Ellis gave a sharp cry.

"You and I were something great once," Merrick said between clenched teeth. "Why can you not remember that? You left and I never questioned it. You came back and now everything is so . . . so wrong."

"Let go!" Ellis begged, but in her panic she could only manage a whisper.

"I let you go once. Now that you're back, I'll never let you go again," Merrick snarled, his grip tightening painfully on her hands.

Ellis tried to pull away. She cried out, "Jenny! Jenny!"

The sound of quick footsteps approached from the parquet floor of the entry.

Merrick released Ellis's hands from his grip in an instant, taking a step back as Ellis fell back to sit once more on the couch.

"Ellis!" Jenny said as she came around through the parlor doors. "I've been simply everywhere looking for Dr. Carmichael, but he isn't— Oh! Merrick! You're here at last! Where is the doctor?"

"He has taken his lodgings up at Hobson's Inn," Merrick said, crossing at once to where Jenny stood. He took up her deformed hands in his own, the picture of gentle sympathy. "I've been doing my best to keep Ellis calm until you returned. I am only sorry the doctor is not here immediately to help. Shall I go and fetch him for you?"

"No," Ellis said at once, standing unsteadily from the couch. "We will not trespass on your hospitality any further. Jenny will see me there."

"Are you sure, Jenny?" Merrick said, the picture of kindness and concern. "I should be happy to oblige."

"That will not be necessary," Ellis interjected before Jenny could speak. "As you say, it is not far."

Jenny looked somewhat crestfallen but nodded.

"Then let me speed you on your errand," Merrick said as he placed his large, strong hand in the middle of each of the ladies' backs and urged them toward the entry. "You had better hurry. The storm will be breaking soon and I would not want a downpour to add to your troubles. Mention my name to Mrs. Hobson and she will accommodate you for the night should the need arise."

"Thank you, Merrick," Jenny said when they reached the door out to the vestibule. "We all depend upon your kindness."

"It's no trouble at all." Merrick nodded as he opened the door for them. "And take care, Ellis. We are all most anxious to hear the results of your examination."

"Good evening, Mr. Bacchus," Ellis said quickly as she ducked out the door with Jenny in tow.

Outside, the wind had picked up as the storm approached, its clouds towering above the Norembega.

"Perhaps we should go back," Jenny suggested.

Ellis fled from the mansion, pretending not to hear her cousin.

Merrick closed the front door of the Norembega and stood silently in the entry hall staring through the glass at the figures retreating from his home.

"Merrick?"

He turned to face the staircase leading down from the second floor.

Alicia was descending the stairs. Her golden hair tumbled down around her shoulders. She wore only a crumpled dress with no stockings.

"Merrick?" she asked again. "What is it?"

"Nothing, Alicia." The master of Gamin cast a disinterested stare in her direction. "Are you certain that is how Ellis looked when she was visited last night?"

The young woman nodded from where she stood on the stairs.

"And the way I touched you," Merrick continued analytically. "It was exactly as Ellis described being touched by the man in the night?"

"Yes. At least it was as Jenny March described it and she heard it directly from Ellis," Alicia said without enthusiasm.

Merrick turned away from her, staring back through the glass of the vestibule.

"Do you think I did it wrong?" Alicia asked, her brow furrowed.

"Jenny may be making up tales," Merrick sniffed.

"Do you need to touch me again?" Alicia asked.

"No," Merrick said at once, his voice heavy. "Go home, Alicia. . . . I have work to do."

14

DOCTOR'S ORDERS

ow, Ellis, there's no need to worry," Dr. Carmichael said in soothing tones.

"No need to worry?" Ellis tried to steady her hands, gripping the edges of her skirt as she struggled to stay still in the chair. "I'm having these thoughts, these nightmares, these dreams, and then I discover them to be made solid and real in my waking life as well? Why should I *not* worry, Doctor?"

"Because there is a simple explanation for all of these, my dear Ellis." Dr. Carmichael sat across from her, leaning forward earnestly and patiently. They sat together in the sunroom on the south side of Hobson's Inn, the shutters drawn against the storm outside and the door securely closed. Mrs. Hobson had allowed the doctor use of space as an examination room for his patients until such time as he could find more suitable accommodations in town, although Ellis wondered anew why the doctor had had a falling-out with Merrick to

the extent that he had felt it necessary to leave the Norembega. "Our minds and our memories are far more fragile than
most of us would like to believe. A little thing can upset them
so radically and you have far more cause than most."

"What cause, Doctor?" Ellis demanded.

"Now, Ellis." Carmichael pulled back, settling against the
back of his chair. "You know you must not push so hard to
recover your memories—"

"No, Doctor," Ellis insisted. "Tell me what has happened
to me. Tell me why I cannot remember my life before except
in nightmares that suddenly threaten me when I'm awake.
Tell me why I dream of roses at night only to cut my feet on
their thorns during the day."

"You know that such things cannot be real," the doctor
said carefully.

"Would you care to examine the cuts?" Ellis replied.

"In due time." The doctor sighed. "I do not doubt that they
are there, my dear girl . . . only how they might have gotten
there. Tell me, do you feel safe here?"

"Whatever do you mean?" Ellis could not stop blinking,
as though there were dust in her eyes that refused to dis-
lodge.

"I mean here in this room." The doctor let his head fall
back to rest against the back of his chair. He gazed at the ceiling, pressing his fingertips together as he spoke. "It's a pleasant place. There are plants in the corners that are tended to by
Mrs. Hobson each day. The lamplight is warm and peaceful.
It is only the two of us here in the room and Jenny is just beyond those closed doors in the parlor. The rain is falling against

the windows, but we're warm and dry in here. So, my question is do you feel safe here in this room?"

Ellis's breathing relaxed into a steady and relaxed rhythm as the doctor spoke. "I suppose I do . . . as safe as anywhere."

Dr. Carmichael smiled sadly. "Then perhaps I may ask you a few questions that may help us both. This dream you had last night . . . do you remember it?"

"Entirely too vividly." Ellis shook visibly.

"You feel certain that you were awake?"

"Yes, I am certain of it."

"I have heard that some dreams can be that way," Dr. Carmichael said as much to himself as to her.

What a strange way of putting it, she thought.

"And in this dream, what were you wearing?"

"My dress."

"Anything else?"

Ellis knitted her brow. "What . . . I don't understand what—"

"Were you wearing anything more than your dress?" the doctor asked, still staring up at the ceiling.

"No shoes or stockings, if that's what you mean." Ellis flushed as she answered. "Really, Doctor, I don't see what this has to do with my problem. Frankly, your examination technique is most peculiar and—"

"Your *case* is most peculiar, Ellis." Carmichael's head snapped forward, his bright eyes fixing on the woman as though to pin her to the back of her chair. "But I think there is a technique that can help you and I believe the time has come to attempt it. It's been used with great effect by those who have studied it under Dr. Bernheim at his school in Nancy—"

"Hypnosis?" Ellis asked.

"No doubt you've heard of it." The doctor smiled, his voice calming and quiet. "Word of this technique has been making its way around my circles with great interest. I believe it would allow us to explore some of those dark corners of your mind, Ellis, shine some light on them and, I trust, help you to properly remember them as well. Do you trust me, too, Ellis? Do you trust Uncle Lucian?"

Ellis's breathing slowed and she sighed deeply. The doctor was looking into her eyes so kindly. "Of course, Doctor."

"Uncle," he corrected.

Ellis smiled. "Yes, Uncle."

Dr. Carmichael leaned forward slowly, taking up her left arm in his right hand as he gazed deeply into her eyes. "Relax, Ellis. You are safe here. Just keep watching me."

He reached up, his hand resting gently on the nape of her neck.

His eyes are such an interesting green.

The world receded.

Her breathing slowed.

Ellis's eyes were closed as she sat in the chair.

Dr. Carmichael's mask of the kindly physician fell as he straightened up to stand before the entranced woman. His green eyes had gone cold as he gazed down at her, considering for a moment what he should do next. It was not a question of what he wanted—it had never been about what *he* wanted—so much as whether he dared to want something for himself at all. He was tired of being here, tired of failing, tired of being forgotten and abandoned. He had come to Gamin full of purpose, but somehow it had gone all wrong and now his patron had abandoned him here.

He had to find a way back into his patron's favor.

Sitting before him was the key to all his problems and he did not know how much time he had to learn what he needed to know.

"Ellis," he said at last after he had made up his mind. "Can you hear me?"

"Yes," she answered with a distant quality in her voice.

"Ellis, I need you to go back in your mind. I need you to remember a time long ago."

"There was a ship," Ellis said, her voice choking as pain crossed her features. "Everyone was running toward the harbor. The children were laughing as they ran down the streets—"

"No, Ellis, before that, long before that," Dr. Carmichael said, impatience seeping into his voice. "Long ago, when you were in Gamin the first time."

"I can't go back." Ellis sighed. "We can never go back. That's what he said. We can only go forward."

"No, no, Ellis," Carmichael urged. "Remember. You were here in Gamin before."

"I wasn't happy." Ellis frowned, her eyes still closed. "I didn't know how to be happy. I didn't know sadness . . . or pain. None of us knew how—"

"Yes, that's right," Carmichael urged. "Where were you when you learned pain, Ellis? Where were you before you learned pain?"

"There . . . I was being chased through a field in the moonlight. There was a creature there in the darkness, a terrible man of shadow, night and talons. There were briars in the dream and a little church that offered me no sanctuary from the monstrous void that followed. And there was a . . . a gate—"

"A gate! Yes!" The doctor leaned forward, resting his hands on her arms, his face within inches of hers. "Tell me about the gate."

"It was bright." Ellis breathed in deeply. "We weren't supposed to play on it."

"Where is the gate, Ellis?" Carmichael insisted, his mouth dry as he spoke the words. "Can you see it?"

"I . . . don't know," she breathed, shaking her head, agitated. "It's hard to see."

"You were there," the doctor seethed. "Tell me what you see!"

"It's so bright and terrible."

"What's around you?" the doctor raged, the locks of his white hair falling down across his reddening face as his frustration mounted. "Don't look at the gate! Tell me what else you see around you!"

"It's too pretty and awful." Ellis pouted beneath her closed eyelids. "Someone moved on the other side. He was so familiar. I couldn't see who he was, so I went closer."

"Go back," the doctor demanded. "Go back further!"

"We can't go back."

"Earlier still, before the gate!"

"We can only go forward. He called me through the gate and said we could only go forward."

"Damnation!" Carmichael stood upright, his fists clenched so tightly that they drained what little color remained from under his papery, pale skin. His breath was ragged as he looked down at his patient.

"Forward it is, then, Ellis," the doctor commanded, his voice hoarse. "Come forward for now, but we'll try again, you and I, to go back. I'll dissect your soul if I must to get my answer. If I have to stake you to a table and take you apart vein by vein, drop by drop and sinew by sinew, I'll have my answer. I'd cut the eyes out of your skull if I could through them see where you have been, my dear. Come forward through the gate and back again . . . back to the train that brought you to me and Summersend and . . ."

Dr. Carmichael paused.

"Back to last night," he said, lowering himself into his chair opposite Ellis, who sat still in her trance. He sneered as he settled into the chair. If he could not get what he wanted from her perhaps he could at least have some amusement. "Back to waking from your slumber. Tell me what happened."

Ellis opened her mouth to speak.

"Better still," the doctor commanded. "*Show* me. . . ."

Ellis tugged at her skirt, which was well above her knees. "I'm sorry, Dr. Carmichael; my mind seems to have wandered."

"It's quite all right, my dear," he said with a pleasant smile. "How do you feel?"

"Why, I feel remarkably better," Ellis admitted with a smile. "Although a bit confused. Is the examination over?"

"Yes, my dear, we are quite finished," Carmichael said as he stood at the sideboard washing his hands in the basin and reaching for the small towel next to it. "The confusion you're feeling is normal for this sort of treatment and I think I can give you a partial diagnosis at this point. Would you like to have Jenny join us for our little talk?"

"Oh yes." Ellis smiled pleasantly. "I'd like that very much."

Dr. Carmichael stepped to the pocket doors, unlatched them and slid one of them back partially into the wall recess. "Jenny, would you care to join us now?"

Jenny slipped through the door past Dr. Carmichael. She rubbed her twisted right hand in front of her with her left, a sure sign that she was worried. "Is it bad news, Uncle Lucian? I've been so worried."

"Not at all," the doctor said, pulling a chair from the corner of the room and setting it down next to Ellis. He motioned for Jenny to sit in it. "In fact, I should say we have made excellent progress."

"Oh, Uncle." Jenny beamed. "That is a relief!"

"Yes, indeed." Dr. Carmichael settled easily into his own chair facing the two young women. "Our dear Ellis is suffering from a condition induced by a traumatic event. These so-called physical manifestations are merely tricks of the brain trying to compensate for recollections and memories which her mind is not yet prepared to face."

"But the rose thorns—"

The doctor smiled gently and held up his hand as he spoke. "Those thorns and the rose were most likely placed there by you, Ellis, and quite possibly that same night as your dream. That you cannot remember them is not surprising; your mind has simply put away that memory. These mysterious appearances and so-called supernatural occurrences are tricks of your own mind. These are phantom memories, created by your mind in the false belief that they are protecting you from the truth."

"But I'm not making these up, Doctor!"

"You *believe* that you are not making these up," Carmichael affirmed. "And in the view of your mind these events are unexplained. What you need to keep in mind is that these things are not real, Ellis; they are only manifestations of your mind trying to heal after witnessing something you're not yet ready to face. Now that we understand the problem, however, we can deal with it. You *do* feel better now, don't you, Ellis?"

Ellis took in a long, deep breath before she answered. "Yes, Uncle, I feel ever so much better."

Jenny looked at Ellis in concern. "Is there anything I can do to help?"

"Yes, Jenny, there is," the doctor said in his most kindly voice. "Help Ellis keep her mind off of her troubles. Some recreational hobbies would be most helpful. It will keep her occupied and allow her mind to heal itself in its own good time."

"Thank you, Uncle," Ellis said as she stood up. "You've been most kind."

"Not at all," Dr. Carmichael replied as he stood as well to bid the young women farewell. "In the meantime, I am always available for additional hypnosis sessions anytime you feel the need."

15

STRIDDLES AND RIDDLES

The needle stabbed up through the cloth. It was a rocking stitch. Ellis concentrated on the needle, gripping it from above and dragging the thread up behind it.

"Not that I know anything about it." Minnie Disir continued to prattle on at length about everything and anything about which she constantly professed to know nothing. She had a weak chin and a small mouth, both of which worked constantly. "But that Ely Rossini has always seemed to me such a serious young man. I thought all young men were supposed to be so carefree."

"They are all worthless gadabouts," Finny said flatly, without looking up from the quilt. The sound of her voice still made Ellis slightly uncomfortable. Finny's weak chin bobbed slightly between the words she muttered. Her dark hair was no longer in the tight bun Ellis remembered from the train but was curled into dark ringlets. The woman had abandoned her nurse's uniform in favor of a simple day dress with a fading pattern and apron. She had apparently not, however, abandoned her brusque manners. "There's not a man in this town worth his salt."

"You are perhaps forgetting Mr. Bacchus?" asked Linny Disir, the third of the three Disir sisters sitting at the frame. She was taller than the other two, with a broader face, and was more contemplative than her siblings.

"Of course I was not referring to Mr. Bacchus." Finny clucked her tongue as she spat out the words. "He has earned his position here in Gamin and no one would say otherwise."

"And what of Dr. Carmichael?" Minnie suggested as she plunged her needle back into the face of the stretched cloth.

"He's an outsider," Finny said dismissively as she stabbed at the quilt. "He doesn't count."

"Well, I don't know," Minnie chattered on. "He's been here a terribly long time."

"So have the soldiers, but you wouldn't consider them one of us," Finny observed.

"Our sister is quite right," Linny said with a nod of her head.

"I understand that the good doctor has had a falling-out with our Mr. Bacchus," Minnie observed. "Moved out of his former lodgings and has ensconced himself over at Hobson's Inn. Although I don't see why he should stay over at Hobson's when we have much better accommodations right here."

"Minnie!" Linny said, setting down her needle at once. The Disirs' large home was known as the Three Sisters' Inn though they rarely took in boarders. "You can see that it would be awkward for the doctor and a continuous nuisance for us. It would be entirely impractical for everyone concerned."

"Still, I have to wonder what transpired between Dr. Carmichael and Mr. Bacchus that would occasion the good doctor's leaving the Norembega. I'm sure I know nothing about it in the slightest, but it is certainly going to be a subject of speculation around the town . . . wouldn't you agree, Miss Martha?"

Ellis glanced up from the needlework of the quilt. In addition to the Disir sisters, Martha, Alicia and Jenny worked intently at the quilt, their needles plunging into the fabric, caught beneath and then thrust upward again through the backing, batting and facecloth like porpoises threading the surface of a fabric ocean. The Gamin Quilters Association met every Thursday afternoon in the front room of the Three Sisters' Inn and considered it a haven for its members from the world beyond the quilting frame.

"Oh yes," Martha replied, her red curls bobbing with every move of her head. "The entire town has been talking about it."

"Well, I don't see why they should." Jenny sat at the end of the frame, just around the corner from Ellis. She, too, was working a needle, although the deformities of her right hand made her work slow and often painful. She rested often and, when she did, fell to talking. "What business is it of ours who Mr. Bacchus invites into his home or dispatches as he pleases? It is his home after all. Nor do I particularly think any of this reflects badly on Uncle Lucian, either; their parting was amicable so far as I know. It may be as simple as they found one another's company tiresome and wanted a fresh start. I think it might be hard for two men in the same home with different habits and sensibilities."

"And what of you, Jenny?" Alicia asked with somewhat exaggerated sweetness. "How are you and Ellis getting by as two women in the same home?"

Concentrate on the needle, Ellis told herself. *Dr. Carmichael said that simple tasks could help you heal. It is a pleasant afternoon, passing the time with kind women gathered around a quilt. What could be more peaceful? More comforting?*

"We couldn't be more content," Jenny affirmed, trying to pick up her needle, but her twisted fingers could not manage it. "Ellis has taken up her painting again. She's improved a good deal since the time she did the little painting in my workroom. She's working on a rather lovely plein air piece of Curtis Island and the lighthouse."

Ellis pricked her finger lightly at the news that she had painted previously. She remembered the garish little ship-wreck painting from that first day when she was trapped in the workroom. But hadn't known till now that it was hers.

"I should very much like to see that!" Martha gushed. "May I come out and watch you paint?"

"You would find it very dull," Ellis said through a gentle smile. "Besides, I'm not very good at all."

"Ellis is being entirely too modest." Jenny left the needle in the cloth, finding it much easier to speak than to attempt the handwork. "It really is fascinating to watch her create something on the canvas. She's also taken up the piano again, although I'll admit that it sometimes makes me a little sad to remember the duets we used to play when we were younger."

"I always admire artists," Minnie chirped. "Of course I don't know a thing about creativity, but it seems like such a marvelous thing to have such a hobby."

"Our Ellis has many unusual hobbies," Alicia said, glancing up from her work to gauge Ellis's reaction. "Including, it seems, the summoning of phantom lovers to her boudoir in the night."

Ellis set her jaw, determined not to rise to the bait.

"Phantom lovers?" Minnie chimed excitedly. "Now that truly is something with which I have no experience!"

The three Disir sisters all laughed as one.

Ellis blushed in spite of herself.

"It was a dream." Jenny giggled. "A delightfully decadent and most provocative dream."

"Another of Ellis's talents." Alicia spoke through a smile, although there was little humor in her tone.

"It's quite unfair, really," Jenny teased. "I'm the one that wants them and *she's* the one that's having them."

"Perhaps that's because she's from the *city*," Alicia said. She was looking intently at Ellis across the quilt now as she lifted the needle and drew the thread up through the quilt. "I understand that this sort of thing happens all the time in the city. Perhaps it was not a dream after all . . . someone might have followed her here *from* the city."

"Striddles and riddles," chided Linny Disir.

"Striddles and riddles," chorused her two sisters.

"Alicia, dear," Linny said, leaning around the corner of the quilting frame, her scissors in hand. "Your thread's looking a bit long . . . may I cut it for you?"

The color drained from Alicia's face. "No, thank you, Miss Linny."

Linny smiled pleasantly, but her eyes carried the warning of an impending storm. "No trouble at all, my dear."

"Has anyone any news of the war in Europe?" Ellis asked, desperately wishing to get the topic of conversation as far from her as possible.

"News of the war?" Martha scoffed. "Why should we trouble ourselves with that?"

"The war is far from Gamin," Finny stated as though her words were the final argument. "It always has been and we prefer it that way."

"But surely you must be concerned with the young servicemen from the town who are in harm's way," Ellis said. "The soldiers—"

"The soldiers are all from out of town," Finny said with some impatience. "None of the young men of Gamin took part in the war nor will they ever if I have anything to say about it!"

"None of them?" Ellis asked with astonishment.

"Oh, we're quite isolationist here." Finny nodded as she plunged her needle through the upper face of the quilt.

"As isolationist as you'll ever find," Minnie added.

"You might say that we're the *original* isolationists," Linny said through a wry smile.

All three of the Disir sisters cackled at this final comment.

Ellis furrowed her brow. "But the soldiers in town are—"

"The soldiers are outsiders." Finny spoke with emphasis as though Ellis may have been hard of hearing. "Have you not been paying attention, child?"

"Fineleah Disir, behave! She simply doesn't understand, is all," Linny said, drawing her own needle up through the quilt. She gazed on Ellis with a cool, patient look. "We like to keep to ourselves. Gamin is a refuge from the troubles out in the world. We don't bother them and would frankly prefer that they not bother us. The city folk don't see it that way. They seem to feel the need to bring their contention and conflict and pain to us and think we'll be happy to accept them. We simply don't want to be bothered. Gamin is a place of rest from such cares. We don't want to be bothered by problems, we don't want to participate in their war and we certainly do not want them bringing such things to our community."

"Gamin is a place of tranquility," Minnie said, her own needle plunging back down into the cloth and being drawn up again in a gentle rhythm. "We let the problems of the outside go their way while we remain constant here and let them drift harmlessly past us. That is why you are here, Ellis. This is a refuge from the problems of the city. You'll understand as soon as you recover. You'll remember why we try to avoid the world and the war and all the problems associated with them."

"It seems to me," Ellis replied, "that everyone here knows more about me than I know of myself. I believe the world is going to intrude on Gamin whether Gamin wishes it or not."

"Be at ease, Ellis," Linny said, her eyes softening as she considered Ellis. "That world is yet very far away. All you need to know for now is that you are home, that here you can rest and that the cares of the world beyond need not trouble you here."

Ellis considered this for a moment. The doctor had said that the only trouble she was having here was of her own making. The strange events she had witnessed were only the attempts of her unraveled mind to knit itself back into a whole. Sun was streaming in through the partially closed blinds at the windows, reflecting off the polished wood floors and floral rugs to fill the room with a warm-toned light. The ladies around the quilting frame occasionally said things that were disturbing, but Ellis was beginning to wonder if it was her own perceptions and imaginings that were the real cause of her own disturbance. Martha, Alicia, the Disir sisters and Jenny were all aglow in the warm morning light of the sitting room, happy as they chatted over the cloth.

I am the only one here who is disturbed, Ellis thought as she finished off her patch of the quilt. *I am the only one upsetting this peaceful place.*

"One last patch to place," Minnie chimed. "You draw it, Ellis."

"Whatever do you mean?" Ellis asked.

"It's a little tradition of ours," Linny explained. "The last patch in a charm quilt will always match the lining of your true love's coat."

"I'd rather not—"

"Oh, but you must!" Martha urged. "It's a great honor among our ladies and a very old tradition."

"You wouldn't want to tempt fate, would you?" Alicia said, her eyes fixed on her handwork. "We insist."

"Oh yes." Jenny smiled. "Please pull the last patch."

"Striddles and riddles." Linny nodded.

"Striddles and riddles," repeated Finny and Minnie.

Ellis reached down into the sack sitting next to the quilting frame determined to get this nonsense over with quickly. Her fingers closed around a piece of cloth. Pulling it free, she thrust it out over the top of the quilt for everyone to see.

Alicia frowned. Martha giggled. Jenny's jaw dropped.

It was a most extraordinary paisley print. Its twisted teardrop shapes of turquoise and gold were set against a deep red background, all in vibrant dyes. The pattern of each paisley shape featured a second paisley within it, which resembled an eye.

"That is entirely unsuitable," Alicia said with a disdainful frown. "The colors don't match any of the other squares of the quilt. It will completely poison the effect of the entire design."

"I think it will make the quilt unique and interesting," Jenny countered, then smiled mischievously. "Besides, the quilt's problems are nothing compared to what Ellis will have to endure. Imagine having to wait so long as to find a man with a red paisley lining in his jacket!"

Martha, Alicia and Minnie laughed at the notion. Even Finny gave a rueful smile.

"Striddles and riddles," Linny said with another pleasant nod.

"Striddles and riddles," chimed in Finny and Minnie.

Ellis set the brightly colored square in its place. It did change the entire complexion of the quilt, yet she found it somehow pleasing in a defiant way. She began working the needle, securing the square to the quilt with firmer, more confident strokes. She was feeling better, she decided. Perhaps her own mind was being pieced back together like this quilt from scraps of memory she was pulling out of some bag at the back of her mind. It was just hard to know when she was sewing in real pieces or those she only imagined. Still, in the comfort of the warm and pleasant parlor in the company of these ladies she felt for the first time in a long while that she was at home.

Her brow furrowed slightly. It seemed odd that the piece she should pull would have the same shape as the mark on her dream man's face.

Don't dwell on it. Fit the patches as they come.

"I've been meaning to ask, Miss Finny," Ellis said, drawing the thread once more through the edge of the paisley patch, "how you managed with that infant. Were you able to get it properly settled?"

"Infant?" Finny frowned. "Whatever are you talking about?"

"The child," Ellis prompted. "The baby that you were accompanying on the train when we came to town."

"You had a baby with you?" Alicia asked, a sudden quality of wonder in her voice. "I would so like to see one. Did you bring it with you from the city?"

"Honestly, both of you!" Finny said. "There was only one person from the city on that train and that was Ellis. There will be no more talk about any baby."

"But all I asked was—"

"There was no baby on that train," Finny said flatly, her eyes fixed on Ellis as she spoke. "The sooner you understand that the sooner you'll find your peace here in Gamin."

"Striddles and riddles," said Linny, nodding.

"Striddles and riddles," repeated her sisters.

The room began to spin around Ellis. She felt dizzy and unwell.

There had been a baby. She had held it. She had sung to it.

Over there, over there, send the word . . .

16

BOOK OF MY DAY

Ellis sat on the back porch of Summersend, the paintbrush motionless in her hand. The canvas rested secure
on the easel before her, but no paint had stroked the surface
in some time. The colors on her palette were drying in the afternoon breeze. The lighthouse remained only sketched on
the surface, vague lines yet to be defined.

Beyond the easel, the porch, lawn, shore and water lay the
lighthouse itself, terribly close and impossibly far away.

Ellis saw nothing of any of them.

She did not trust anything that she saw or heard.

"Ellis?"

The voice was soft and gentle. She knew the voice but
could not be certain it was real.

"Ellis, dear, please talk to me."

Jenny's gnarled right hand closed clumsily over her own.
Ellis stared at it for a while, wondering at it. The fingers were

broken in multiple places, she observed. The proximal phalanx and middle phalanx of the index and second fingers had
healed improperly due to the shattering of the bones, which
looked to be comminuted. There appeared to be some distress of the tendons—flexor digitorum profundus—and the
metacarpal bones may have been fractured as well. None of
them looked to have been properly set.

Ellis drew in a deep breath. *How do I know all that? And
what kind of doctor was Uncle Lucian that he could not have taken
care of her injury when it happened? And if that was the extent of his
medical knowledge, then what kind of treatment am I receiving at his
hands?*

"See, Ellis," Jenny continued. "I brought you a rose—a
white one from the garden. You like white roses."

Ellis turned slowly toward the rose, her eyes fixing on it. It
took her at once back to her own bedroom, the shadowy man
who had become real among the cloud of moths. His touch,
his longing, his despair all drawing on her soul until fear burst
out of her and scattered him into the storm of the night. He
had brought her a rose just as white with thorns just as sharp.
It had been a nightmare that proved too real the next day on
her bloodstained stocking.

*Hold still and everything will sort itself out. Hold still and the dust
clouds will settle.*

"What am I to do with you?" Jenny sighed. "You've been
this way since we returned from the quilting society. I thought
your paints might have brought you out of this. Where are you,
Ellis?"

Where am I? Do I know?

Jenny knelt down in front of Ellis. She took the paintbrush from her with her left hand and carefully set it down at the base of the easel. She winced once from the pain in her leg but continued despite the discomfort.

"Ellis, what if I were to show you something special?" Jenny whispered as though the breeze might carry her words across the bay waters and into town. "Something secret . . . something I'm not supposed to show to anyone?"

Ellis tried to focus on Jenny's large eyes.

"Something I'm especially not supposed to show to you?"

Ellis parted her parched lips, managing somehow to force out the mirrored words. "Not supposed to show me?"

Jenny smiled, encouraged by the thought that she was getting through to Ellis. "Yes! Would that please you?"

Ellis paused for a moment and thought, *What are they hiding from me? They must be hiding something.* "Of course, Jenny. What do you want to show me?"

A moment of uncertainty crossed Jenny's features, but she continued, "Well . . . we have to go inside. The workroom, perhaps, would be safe enough."

Jenny stood up slowly and then moved quickly through the screen door into the breakfast nook. The door banged shut behind her as she moved quickly into the labyrinthine interior of the house.

Ellis stood up, her focus returning outward as she wondered what Jenny could possibly produce that was supposed to be kept secret especially from her. She pulled the screen door open and stepped inside.

She moved through the archway into the grand salon at

the back of the house. The double doors to the rotunda were open at the top of the landing. Jenny stood in the archway holding open one of the odd bookcase doors that led into the workroom.

"Come, Ellis, this way," Jenny whispered, although Ellis could hardly think that anyone was within shouting distance of the house. Ellis took the single step up onto the landing and moved quickly through the double doors and behind the bookcase beyond.

The workroom was as Ellis remembered it, pristine and fresh as though no work had ever been done in it. She heard Jenny swing the door quietly closed behind them.

"Cover your eyes, Ellis." Her cousin appeared as nervous as a cat.

"Honestly, Jenny." Ellis shook her head in puzzlement. "What is so mysterious that—"

"It's important, Cousin," Jenny insisted, her eyelids blinking quickly as she spoke.

"Very well." Ellis shrugged, putting her hands up to cover her eyes. "But I really don't understand what all the fuss is about."

Jenny moved about the room. There was a scraping sound and a high-pitched squeal as though metal was being dragged across the floor. A few more scraping sounds followed.

"Open your eyes, Cousin!" Jenny murmured.

Ellis looked.

The room was identical to how she last remembered it, perfectly ordered, with all the cabinets shut. Jenny stood before her holding an object out with her trembling hands.

Ellis almost laughed. She had steeled herself to anticipate something unexpected, but the utterly ordinary quality of the object took her aback.

"It's a scrapbook, Jenny," Ellis said with a nonplussed look.

"It's *my* book," Jenny said, her eyes bright though her lips were trembling. "This is the *Book of My Day.*"

Ellis reached out, taking the book. It left Jenny's hands reluctantly. The cover was cloth over the boards and binding, a canvas that looked as though it might once have been from a sail. There were shells affixed to the cover around a fading print of a ship fighting her way through rough seas. Bits of rough rope edged the book cover. These held a burgeoning, thick set of pages that threatened to split the binding.

"I don't understand," Ellis said, handing the thick book casually back to Jenny.

"Well, let me show it to you." Jenny snatched the book back, a confused look crossing her face. She set the book down on the table next to the sewing machine, carefully opening the cover to the first page. "See, here is Gamin . . . the whole bay and Curtis Island Lighthouse, too. That's where we'll start out."

The pages open before them were nearly overflowing with snippets and decoration. There was a central print of Gamin that looked as though it was looking out from somewhere on the waters of the bay. A three-masted ship had been cut out and pasted on top of the picture so that she might look as though she were sailing. There were cutouts of people, too, who were set as though they were standing on the shore, their heads replaced by woodcut portraits of Merrick, Martha, Ely and Silenus. The forms of two women in dresses were pasted to the back of the ship, each with cutout photographic prints of Ellis's and Jenny's heads set atop them. That area of the ship's image was rough as though something had been pasted there before and had been replaced by the images of the two women. The size and perspectives were all wrong and the effect was both comical and somewhat unnerving.

"That's us," Jenny said proudly. "We'll lead everyone out of the harbor and to the open water beyond and go anywhere we want!"

"That sounds wonderful," Ellis said cautiously, uncertain as to where all this was leading. "And where would we go?"

"Oh, here!" Jenny breathed, her eyes shining as she turned the thick page to the next spread. "We would sail on the open waters to amazing places."

Ellis looked down to the page before them. A waving ribbon of blue had been affixed across the page. There was another print of a ship here, this one from a painting. Another pair of grossly exaggerated figures representing Ellis and Jenny were glued to the back of the ship. Pieces of muslin clouds swept across the tops of the pages. The ocean shone back at Ellis as a thin scrap of brushed tin. Seagulls cut from snippets of feathers rode the implied breeze above the masts. Smaller figures, again disproportionate, stood in the front of the ship.

"These are Merrick, Martha, Ely and Silenus." Ellis pointed toward the figures standing in the ship's bow.

"Yes." Jenny nodded with a thoughtful smile. "They'll be coming with us."

"And the others?" Ellis asked quietly. "Where are they?"

Jenny's smile fell, her brows knitting slightly at a memory. "They come on a different boat. When it's my day then I'll have it the way I want it."

Jenny turned the page again. As she did the metallic ocean seemed to move and Ellis thought for a moment she could smell a fresh sea breeze, but the new pages were already before her. Page after page swept past Ellis. Absurd pirate ships attacking without reason or result, islands with three trees and filled with people calling for help, treasure hunts among cannibals . . . it was all a child's view of what lay beyond the horizons of Penobscot Bay. Ellis found it both charming and disturbing that her cousin should know so little of the world beyond Gamin.

"And where will we stop?" Ellis asked with a gentle tone.

"Oh, anywhere we want!" Jenny replied cheerfully.

"But *where* would you like to stay?" Ellis urged.

"Oh, it doesn't matter." Jenny smiled. "Just so long as I have my day."

"What about, say, Boston or Halifax or even Bristol?"

"The city?"

Ellis blinked. "Yes, wouldn't you like to see a city? We could sail there on your ship."

"Oh no." Jenny shook her head. "I'm not ready for the city . . . not yet. That's what Captain Walker says, anyway. Of course, Merrick doesn't want me to go to the city at all. . . ."

"Captain Walker?" Ellis asked.

"Yes, he brought his own ship into Gamin a while back." Jenny nodded. "He came on a storm like the one we had the other night— Oh, I'm sorry, Ellis; I didn't mean to—"

"It's all right," Ellis assured her. "What about Captain Walker?"

"Isaiah?" Jenny beamed. "His ship was driven aground against Curtis Island a few years back. Sank there with all hands lost save him only. He said he came from a terrible place across the water and that he was glad to have made the harbor here in Gamin. He told me all about the sea. I used to listen to him for hours even though none of us were supposed to talk to him."

Now the ocean on the page was a violent and raging black satin. The ship was different yet again, this one a woodcut print of a two-masted schooner pushed hard over in a gale. The strange figures were again on the ship in exaggerated size, this time represented by cloth dolls. Monstrous creatures made of burlap, seashells, buttons and charms rose up to threaten the vessel while foil lightning crashed downward from a gray linen sky. This time there were other dolls depicted as being in the black water.

"Won't it be exciting, Ellis?" Jenny smiled as she turned the page again.

The storm from the previous pages continued. This ship was from a different woodcut print but sailing away from Ellis. On the horizon, just peeking above it, was a broken glass button shining brightly against the darkness of the page. Threads of gold reached out from the broken glass like the rays of hope at the end of the storm. The ship, carrying a single figure, sailed toward the light.

"Only one aboard?" Ellis asked.

Jenny flushed. "It's why I took the book from the Night-birds Society. I needed to fix it before I put it back. That's why I took it from the literary society and brought it home."

"You keep your scrapbook at the society?" Ellis was astonished.

"Well, we all keep them there," Jenny said. "Everyone here in Gamin has one! Everyone wants to have their day. You'll have one, too, and when you do you'll—"

A distant knocking froze Jenny midsentence.

"Ellis? Jenny?" The sound was muted by the walls.

"It's Merrick!" Jenny breathed, terror on her face. "He can't find out I've got my book here! You've got to get out and distract him. Send him away, Ellis, please!"

Ellis tried to calm her cousin. "If we just wait quietly, perhaps he'll go away. Then we can—"

"He won't." Jenny was in a near panic. "He'll come in and trap us in this room!"

"Ellis! Where are you?" Merrick's voice was growing more insistent. There were other voices, lower and less distinct, that could be heard as well.

"Why did you ever design a room like this!" Ellis fumed. "It's a trap, Jenny!"

"Me?" Jenny was incensed. "This design was entirely *your* idea!"

The muffled, distant sound of the front-porch door slamming came through the walls.

"Ellis? Jenny?" Several voices now called out their names. A woman's voice was distinguished from the men's.

Jenny was shaking, staring at the patch of blank wall through which she and Ellis had entered the workroom from the rotunda arch beyond.

Ellis stepped over to the section of wall next to it where the second door was located. The latch was still open as she pushed on it. The bookcase swung outward and Ellis slipped quickly into the music room. She hesitated for a moment but was relieved to see that the double doors that led to the vestibule were still shut. Ellis crossed to the doors and pulled them open.

"Mr. Bacchus!" she called out as she stepped into the vestibule. "I am rather surprised to find you in my home, sir."

Merrick, standing in the arch at the far side of the rotunda, turned from the vase on the bookshelf with a look of puzzled surprise on his face. Alicia and Ely both stood in the rotunda and looked relieved to see Ellis in the vestibule behind them.

"My apologies for not answering you earlier, but I was engaged here in the music room," Ellis said. "I'm afraid I was carried away in my reveries and did not hear your knock."

"Of course," Ely said at once. "Quite understandable."

Merrick's gaze fixed on Ely for a moment before returning to Ellis. "We were concerned when you did not answer."

"Jenny is indisposed at the moment," Ellis said at once. "I must beg you to leave the house. I do not wish to disturb her rest."

Merrick stepped away from the bookcase in the archway and strolled casually toward Ellis across the parquet floor of the rotunda. He passed between Ely and Alicia without a glance. "I am sorry to hear Jenny is unwell. Strange, though, that you should have taken ill at the quilting today and now it is Jenny who needs to recover."

"We have an invitation to deliver," Alicia said quickly. "Once that's done, we'll not trespass on you further."

"Yes," Ely said, licking his lips. "Only please say you'll come."

"An invitation?" Ellis asked.

"Yes," Merrick said. He was standing uncomfortably close to Ellis once again, as though he had a right to her space. "Alicia and Ely both feel you are in need both of welcoming and cheering up. They propose a soiree this evening in your honor."

"There'll be dancing," Alicia said, an urgent pleading in her voice.

"And music," Ely added insistently.

"I have offered the use of my home for the occasion," Merrick said, gazing down at Ellis. "I trust you'll save a dance for me?"

"But may I beg the honor of your first dance?" Ely added at once. "Please do not disappoint me."

Ellis thought of Jenny panicking in the workroom. She had to get these people out of the house, although why Jenny should be so upset over a scrapbook she did not fathom.

"Please say you'll come." Alicia bit at her lower lip.

"Of course," she answered. "What time are we expected?"

17

SOIREE

*I*sn't it beautiful!" Jenny exclaimed as they stepped up the stairs and onto the veranda at the back of the Norembega.

Ellis remained thoughtful. The veranda overlooked a terrace below. Chinese lanterns had been strung along cables that were, in turn, suspended from poles placed at intervals around the terrace. Wide iron cauldrons had also been set about the terrace, their coals and wood providing welcome if somewhat localized relief from the chill in the air. The Victrola from the literary society blared the poorly reproduced sounds of a Scott Joplin rag from one corner where a number of couples were dancing. The crowd covering the wide terrace spilled out onto the large lawn that ran down the slope affording an unhindered view of Gamin Bay. The beam of the lighthouse on Curtis Island stood out clearly against the twilight of the horizon, its beam sweeping like a searching eye.

It called to Ellis.

"Ellis?" Jenny prodded.

"Oh, I'm sorry," she replied, shaking herself from her reveries. "What were you saying?"

"You *are* distracted." Jenny laughed. "Well, a good party will set you to rights. Diversion is always a good cure for distraction, I always say."

Jenny took Ellis by the right hand and led her to one of the two facing flights of stairs that gave access down from the veranda at the back of the house to the terrace just below.

In moments they had descended into the milling crowd. Ellis had shared with Jenny one of the party dresses from her trunk and her cousin had been most anxious to show it off from the moment she had seen it. Now, however, as Ellis moved through the crowd, she found no familiar faces among them. As the soiree had been given in her honor, she had expected the guest list to have included someone she had met before—

But, she reminded herself, *you don't really know anybody.* Still, she would have thought that some of the faces in the crowd would be recognizable from the Nightbirds Literary Society or Jenny's friends who occasionally called at Summersend. There were no soldiers present so far as Ellis could see and, for that matter, Dr. Carmichael's scarecrow visage was absent as well. She would have even welcomed seeing the rather sour face of Finny Disir. Yet both Ely and Alicia had been so insistent that Ellis come. Surely they must be here somewhere in the throng.

The laughing, roaring horde pressed close about as Jenny tried to lead them across the terrace from the base of the stairs. The Joplin rag had ended and been replaced rather incongruously with a waltz. The crowd around them shifted, jostling them suddenly. Jenny's grip slipped from Ellis's hand. Almost at once Ellis lost sight of her cousin in the throng.

"Jenny!" Ellis called out, but her words were swallowed up by the laughter, chatter and shrieking of the mob about her. "Jenny!"

Someone firmly gripped Ellis's hand, pulling her sideways through the crowd and into the more open, welcoming expanse of the dance floor.

Ely, she thought gratefully as she blindly stumbled onto the floor. *His first dance.*

She followed the lead with the lift of her hand, pirouetting under the arm and emerging into a classic dance hold.

It was not Ely.

She was staring with suddenly wide eyes into the face of the man of her nightmares.

He wore a charcoal gray military greatcoat of worsted wool with the cape still attached, but if there had ever been rank insignia or service pins adorning it they had been removed. He wore no cap. His carefully combed hair was dark and wavy. His eyes were of a gray-green color that she found compelling, but they spoke to her of a sadness and longing of such depths that it frightened her. He had a face of that type that was perpetually youthful at any age.

But it was the paisley-shaped bruise that surrounded his right eye and arched across his forehead that made her tremble.

The waltz spun its opening bars across the terrace with scratchy tones from the Victrola.

The Nightmare Man pressed lightly with his right hand while pulling her waist with his left.

Transfixed, Ellis spun with him into the small world of their dance.

"Do you know me?" he asked with hope.

Passion. Heat. Pain. Desire. Giving. Taking. Holding. Fear. His voice called up thoughts and impressions unbidden. *Terrible. Familiar.*

"Who are you?" Ellis gasped as all of Gamin whirled around them.

"I am Jonas," he said.

Ecstasy. Trembling. Anger. Betrayal. Tears.

"No. I don't know you." She knew it was a lie even as she spoke the words.

He knew it, too. He smiled even as his eyes welled up with tears.

"You have known me forever," Jonas said as they whirled among the dancers on the floor. "I have loved you since before you breathed your first breath. I love you still and I've crossed heaven and hell to bring you back."

"I just *came* back!"

"This isn't where you belong."

"I *do* belong here!"

"Not anymore," he said, the world spinning in the distance beyond them. "I failed you once before. I am so sorry—more sorry than I can say—but I swear I will never fail you again. I've come to free you from this place forever."

"Like you freed those women in Halifax or Bar Harbor, I suppose," Ellis insisted. "Or that artist woman here in Gamin. I'll not be going anywhere with you, sir!"

"This isn't the life you're meant to live," Jonas insisted. "You need to live, Ellis . . . and I can help you live again."

"Live *again*?" Ellis felt a chill run through her as she said the words. "So you see me as dead already?"

"No." Jonas smiled. "Not yet, but very soon if—"

Jonas suddenly flew backward. Ellis, released from their dance hold, stumbled, turning once before she regained her footing.

Merrick held Jonas by the collar of his greatcoat. The tall man hooked his foot behind Jonas's ankle and threw him back down onto the stones of the terrace.

Someone stopped the music.

Ely and Alicia pushed their way through the stunned partygoers and hurried to Ellis's side.

"His face! Just as you described it!" Alicia said in a hushed whisper. "Who is he, Ellis?"

"I . . . I d-d-don't know," Ellis stammered.

"This is a private function, Lieutenant." Merrick seethed as he stood between the prostrate Jonas and where Ellis stood trying to catch her breath. "I was most clear that soldiers were not welcome at this event or ever, for that matter, at my home. And need I add that it is the law in Gamin that soldiers be in uniform at all times. Now I find that these very distinct instructions have been lost on you."

Jonas struggled to his feet, rubbing his chin. He unbuttoned his greatcoat, pulling it open. As he extended his arms, the panels of the coat opened up like wings.

The lining of the coat had been rendered in silk paisley.

"As you can see, I am in uniform," Jonas said. Beneath the paisley-lined greatcoat he wore an officer's jacket with a leather belt and shoulder strap. His jodhpurs and jacket, however, both bore dark stains and dirt. "I see that you have also banished Dr. Carmichael from your gathering. At least your prejudices are evenhanded, Merrick."

"Get out, *Lieutenant*." Merrick spat the last word with distaste. "You're not welcome here."

"Welcome or not, I've come for her," Jonas said, pointing at Ellis.

"She's come home," Merrick said, shaking his head. "You're an outsider and cannot possibly think that you have any authority here."

"She was mine," Jonas insisted.

"She was mine first," Merrick countered. "You're a thief. Your stolen goods were returned to their rightful place and now you whine that the property you stole is no longer yours. But this is *my* day, Jonas. My rules. My law."

"I'm not bound by your law," Jonas replied. "I've come for her, Merrick . . . and nothing is going to stop me!"

Merrick leaped toward Jonas with a cry. His grasp closed around the collar of the greatcoat as Jonas turned. The coat sagged.

Moths, hundreds in various sizes and shapes, erupted from the collar of the coat, rushing upward into the deepening night sky.

Silence gripped the crowd.

Ellis trembled between Alicia and Ely, the world growing distant as she felt she was about to faint.

Merrick turned, the now-empty coat still held up in his grip.

A broad smile came to his face.

"Magic!" Merrick declared with a laugh. "Abracadabra! I've made the bogeyman disappear!"

Tittering laughter sprinkled through the crowd.

"I hope you all enjoyed our little entertainment." Merrick beamed, waving the greatcoat as though it were a matador's cape. The laughter grew as Merrick posed with the coat, flicking it for his audience. Soon applause ensued and a few cheers. Merrick took a bow. "I may not be Houdini, but I trust our little drama was diverting!"

Ellis was not applauding, nor, she realized, were Alicia and Ely next to her. Above Merrick's smile Ellis noticed his brow was glistening. The man was sweating.

Jenny emerged at last from the cheering mob, excited and flushed. "Ellis, was that the man you saw in your dream?"

"Yes." Ellis nodded, trying to swallow, but her mouth had suddenly gone quite dry.

"Of course, it couldn't have been the man in your dream, really," Jenny went on. "I mean, it must have all been part of Merrick's clever little performance."

"There was nothing clever about it!" Ellis snapped at

Jenny. "Even if he had arranged such a thing, it would have been a cruel joke!"

"I'm sure he meant well," Jenny said, taken suddenly aback. "Really, Ellie, I know that Merrick can sometimes do things that make him appear difficult, but he has our best interests at heart."

"Does he?" Alicia demanded. "Don't you *ever* question him?"

"Why should I?" Jenny answered. "It's his day and I honor it as we all should."

Merrick took another bow and then raised his hand in a beckoning gesture. "Let the party continue. Strike up the music once more, my good friends. I feel like a nice Castle Walk."

The Victrola screeched back to life as the needle dropped back into the recorded groove. It was another Joplin ragtime dance—the "Pleasant Moments" rag—and the dancers returned to the floor moving at once into a Castle Walk step. It was a simple step, Ellis observed, one easily taught to the inexperienced.

Merrick tossed the greatcoat over a lawn chair at the edge of the dance floor and strode up to where Ellis was standing. Jenny brightened considerably as he approached, but her expression fell as Merrick ignored her and spoke directly to Ellis.

"I see that my little play has upset you," Merrick said, holding out his hand by way of invitation. "Perhaps I can make amends by—"

"I believe Miss Harkington has promised her first dance to me," Ely interrupted.

"But Ellis has already danced," Merrick said, casting a cool eye on the young man.

"I hardly think that the unwanted attentions of a masher should qualify for the first dance of the evening," Ely said, taking up Ellis's hand.

"I'm sure that Miss March will be delighted to be your partner, Merrick," Alicia added. "Then when Mr. Rossini has returned with Ellis she will be delighted to take a turn around the floor with you."

Jenny beamed up at Merrick.

"Miss Harkington?" Ely urged.

"Mr. Rossini." Ellis nodded as she moved in front of him to take up her dancing position.

Ely gave gentle pressure with his hand and Ellis stepped back with the beat. They quickly merged with the other couples on the floor, Merrick staring after them in their wake.

"Mr. Rossini," Ellis said, "thank you for being kind, but did you *see* that man with the paisley-shaped—"

"We have not much time," Ely said, his words quick and clipped. "Can you show us the gate?"

"Show you the . . . what gate?"

"We have to get out," Ely continued. "I've been trying for some time. I've listened to the soldiers and spoken with Dr. Carmichael, but I don't want the responsibility that either of them demands. Alicia and I both want to get out—the same way you did—and you're the only one who can show us the way."

"Out?" Ellis was feeling dizzy again. "Out from where?"

"Here!" Ely insisted even as they both continued the precise steps around the floor. "Gamin!"

"But why?" Ellis asked. "You seem so happy here—"

"It's a prison, Ellis," Ely said. "I'm tired of pretending at life. . . . I want to live it like you did."

"Like I *did*?" Something cold and hard formed inside of her.

"All you need to do is show us the way you left," Ely said.

"But I don't *remember* leaving," Ellis said. "I don't remember anything!"

"Well, how did you get back?" Ely asked. "You were away . . . in the city. . . . How did you get here?"

"On the train," Ellis said. "It's the first thing I remember with any clarity at all: waking up on the train."

"Then that's where we'll start," Ely said. "Alicia is arranging it so that Merrick will be occupied for some time. Alicia will join us on the south side of the house and we'll leave at once."

"Leave?" Ellis was shocked. "Why should I leave?"

"Because none of this makes any sense to you, does it?" Ely said. "Because you're not insane—they only want you to think you are. And mostly, Ellis, you should show us the way because none of this madness will stop until you do."

"What about Jenny?" Ellis asked.

"Show us the way out," Ely said, "and then you can save Jenny, too."

18

TWISTED RAILS

Their carriage plunged down High Street. Ellis sat wedged into the seat with Ely clutching the reins on her left and Alicia gripping one of the steel bow sockets supporting the top on their right. Ely glanced nervously behind them from time to time, sweat breaking out on his brow despite the chill of the evening air rushing past them. The lights from the party at the Norembega fell behind them, the sounds of it fading into the clatter of the horses' hooves and the rumble of the narrow tires below. The canvas top swayed above them in their headlong rush. The road was bright before them under a rising moon and the pools of light from the occasional gas lamps on either side. Porch lights, too, illuminated the scene from the homes on either side. It all struck Ellis as potentially idyllic if the company with her crammed into the seat of the carriage were not so desperate.

Ely pulled on the reins, his foot pressing hard against the

dash. The horse raised her head, whinnying in protest as she cut to the right, the carriage sliding across the gravel covering the access road. The carriage tipped slightly before righting itself.

The train station lay just ahead.

"It's your fault," Alicia said to Ellis, both anger and fear edging her words. "There was no reason for you to bring Jonas here. No doubt he was perfectly well off where he was and now all you've done is upset everyone!"

"Jonas!" Ellis exclaimed. "I didn't bring him here!"

"This isn't a game anymore," Alicia snapped. "You could have sent Jonas back and everything could have stayed just the way it was—for his own sake and everyone else's. But you had to bring him here and ruin it all!"

"It will be all right," Ely said, easing up on the reins as the brightly lit platform of the train station loomed before them. "Just as soon as she shows us the way through the gate, we should be safe."

"Safe?" Ellis asked. "Safe from what?"

The horse slowed to a trot. Ely pulled the carriage around to the front of the southernmost platform and dropped the reins. He reached his foot down for the long step mounted to the side of the carriage and swung his other foot down to the ground. He dashed around the back of the carriage to the opposite side, lifting Alicia down. Ellis moved to step down from the carriage herself, but Ely lifted her clear of the vehicle's body and placed her on the ground. He gripped her hand and pulled her up the steps toward the station.

The platform was utterly deserted beneath the brilliant

210 TRACY HICKMAN & LAURA HICKMAN

light of the gas lamps. There was freight on the platform and several pieces of luggage but not a single passenger or freight handler. The locomotive chuffed just beyond the southern end of the platform, smoke billowing from its stack and steam hissing from its vents. There was a baggage car behind the tender and four Pullman cars making up the rest of the train. No conductors wandered the station platform. No faces looked out from the windows of the train.

"Let's go," Ely said, pulling Ellis toward the train.

"Wait!" Ellis said. "Where are we going?"

"That's what you're supposed to tell us," Alicia said, biting at her lower lip again. "This isn't going to work, Ely!"

"Ellis made it, didn't she?" Ely argued. He pulled Ellis up the stairs into the Pullman car. "Come on!"

Alicia followed at once.

The Pullman car was brightly lit and, like the platform, completely empty. Ely pulled Ellis behind him, his hand gripping hers painfully hard, until they reached the middle of the car. He swung her over toward a cushioned chair. Alicia sat down next to her. Ellis looked down at her party dress and at the empty railroad car around them.

"Ely, this is ridiculous," Ellis said, moving to stand up.

The train lurched suddenly, forcing Ellis to sit down at once. The station platform began to slip past the windows of the Pullman.

"All right," Ely said, leaning forward toward Ellis. "That's as much as I can do."

"I'd say you have done quite enough!" Ellis sputtered. "This has gone far beyond games, Ely! This is kidnapping!"

The lit platform of the station fell behind them as the train picked up speed. The dark silhouettes of the trees increasingly blocked the lights of Gamin and the moonlight shining on the bay beyond.

"She's useless to us," Alicia said in exasperation. "I told you, Ely. . . . I was there."

"No," Ely said, shaking his head. "Please, Ellis, you've got to remember. We can help you—we will help you—but you have to help us first! The gate, Ellis. What do you remember about the gate?"

"Nothing," Ellis said, shaking her head.

"She's forgotten," Alicia moaned. "It's no use."

"Listen to me, Ellis. You and Merrick had a fight," Ely continued. "You both were so stubborn and he has a fearsome temper. One day the rage was too much for you and you went from Gamin and never returned. It's not there anymore, but if you can just remember what it was like—"

She could not see it at first. She was so very angry and upset.

Ellis blinked. There was a flash of a memory, an impression of light that called to her.

A field in the moonlight. Her tears in the moonlight. Away. Far away where he would not look for her.

"I . . . I d-d-don't know," Ellis stammered.

Beyond Gamin. They walked the fields. The sun had fallen from her right hand.

"Were you on the train?" Ely urged. "Please, Ellis! Think!"

A church hidden among the trees. The Children's Church.

The clattering of the rails continued as the train followed the tracks straight toward the south.

"Where is it, Ellis?" Ely demanded. "You're the only one who can find it. Where is it?"

"A very good question," came a voice from the vestibule at the back of the railcar.

Ely's head jerked up at the sound. Ellis and Alicia both turned suddenly.

"Indeed, the very question I've been asking for some time." Dr. Carmichael stood leaning against the frame of the door, swaying slightly with the motion of the car. His boater hat was pushed back onto his head. His waistcoat was unbuttoned beneath his open coat. His tie was missing and his collar undone at the top. "By all means, Ellis, where did you go that day?"

Ellis sat silent as the wheels of the railcar clacked rhythmically along the rails.

"Wherever it was, it certainly wasn't on this train," Dr. Carmichael stated with a malevolent smile. "I know this train very well. This train might arrive from just about anywhere, but it only has one destination now."

Ellis opened her mouth to speak, but Ely spoke to her first. "We cannot trust him, Ellis. He is an 'outsider'—not like us—and he's siding with Merrick in the game."

"It is true that I've taken sides but not with Merrick." Carmichael shrugged. "I don't expect you to understand, my dear Ellis, but we all want the same thing—to get away from this lovely, perverted gilded cage. It is, after all, why I followed you since you left the party although I above all people here could tell you this railroad excursion would not work. Nevertheless, I may still be able to help."

"You've never helped anyone," Ely said, his face gone suddenly pale.

"Well, it's not for a lack of trying," Dr. Carmichael answered. "You know there was a time when I could help you leave here anytime you chose. Interesting phrase that, don't you think . . . 'anytime you chose'? I could have taken you to a place right on this very train where you never have to worry again, never have to deal with the burdens of your decisions or the consequences of your actions. It wouldn't have cost you anything that's of any real use to you and we would have ridden these very rails there together. All I would have asked was that you put in a good word for me when you get to your destination and ask my master if I might be allowed to perform some other service—*any* other service—on his behalf. But Gamin certainly has changed, hasn't it, Ely? The rails have all gone twisted now. But there certainly was a time when I could have taken you away."

"We are not choosing sides in your war," Alicia said flatly. "We never wanted any part of it. We just want—"

"You just want to enjoy the fruits without working the harvest." Carmichael sneered. "You just want to ride the ride at your carnival without paying for the ticket. Don't we all?"

"If you're so anxious about our leaving," Alicia said, thrusting out her jaw in defiance, "then why are you trying to stop us?"

"Oh, my dear Alicia Van der Meer." The doctor smiled as he stepped forward and took his own seat across the aisle from them. He leaned back. "I don't want to stop you. Quite the contrary; I want to go *with* you. You see, we're a great deal more alike than you think. In my case, however, I keep paying for the ticket without ever getting to go on the ride."

"We appear to already be going somewhere," Ellis said as the train plunged southward down the line.

"Perhaps we have already arrived?" Carmichael sighed with a sad nod of his head.

The train whistle blew. The rhythm of the rails slowed its pace. The train was coming to the next stop.

"You're all as mad as a March Hare and I'm tired of being the goat of your cruel jokes! I'm getting off," Ellis announced, "and taking the next train back to Gamin."

Alicia's eyes were fixed outside the window as light from the station began to fill the slowing Pullman car. "I don't think that will be necessary, Ellis."

Ellis turned to the window.

The train was slowing next to the station. Gas lamps brightly illuminated the empty station platform and the large sign over the double doors into the building in its center.

The sign read GAMIN.

"But . . . we couldn't be back!" Ellis exclaimed. "The train traveled in a straight line. There were no turns!"

"Jenny can only hold Merrick's attention so long," Alicia said. "We should call this off, Ely . . . hurry back to the party and hope no one has missed us!"

"No!" Ely insisted. "I've been sent to the Umbra before and I won't go back. We're getting out of here."

An unearthly howl suddenly shook the Pullman car. Its power raised dust up from around the railroad platform outside and caused the station-house sign to swing on its hooks.

It was mournful, desperate and hungry. There was something basic and animal in the trumpeting that shook Ellis to her bones.

Worse, it was familiar to her.

The familiarity terrified her.

The sound died away into the distance, leaving a profound silence in the still Pullman car.

"Now, there's something we haven't heard for a long time," Dr. Carmichael said, drawing in a deep breath. He removed his boater hat, shook his head and sighed.

Ellis struggled to think.

The howl resounded again, closer somehow this time. Several of the glass panes in the Pullman car cracked at the sound.

"You should have sent him away," Alicia wept. "Now it's too late! You've ruined it for us all!"

Ely grabbed Ellis by her shoulders, shouting into her face, "We've got to run, Ellis! We've got to find the gate before that thing finds us."

"What's happening?" Ellis blinked. "What kind of hell is this?"

"Hell? Oh, Ellis, you've got it wrong. This isn't hell." Ely grinned maniacally. "This is where they send those who aren't *good* enough for hell!"

"Welcome home, everyone." Dr. Carmichael set his feet up on the seat in front of him and doffed his hat in his private, scornful joke. "Again."

19

THE GATE

Ely ran across the railroad platform, dragging Ellis behind him, her hand crushed in his desperate grip. Alicia followed behind, tears streaming down her face. The carriage was gone, the horse having bolted at the first monstrous trumpeting sound. Ely did not miss a step. He plunged across the lawn, cutting the corner of the access road in his dash toward High Street. Ellis struggled to keep her footing as the folds of her party dress threatened constantly to trip her. The grass stained the hem as she ran. She could hear Alicia's breath behind her, gasps for air driven by fear. Ellis's heart pounded inside her chest.

High Street was deserted.

The bellowing howl thundered down the street from their left. Alicia gave a short scream, but it was swallowed up by the cacophony of rage that shook the ground under their feet. The sound washed past them like a tidal wave.

"This way!" Ely shouted, pulling Ellis behind him south down High Street.

"Town?" Alicia asked, following after them both. "You think the town will protect you?"

"We need time!" Ely shouted back. "There's someone there who can help."

"Against that?" Ellis struggled to keep her feet under her.

They hurried past the Nightbirds Literary Society House and toward the center of Gamin. Ely cut across the empty street toward the burned-out buildings, kicking down a charred door and motioning them all inside. The smell of charred wood and paint filled Ellis's nostrils. Her eyes began to water. Ely did not stop, however, urging them farther into the building's devastation and the back storerooms. The wood creaked beneath their feet, soot coating Ellis's and Alicia's party shoes, smudging their dresses and gloved hands. The second-story floor had collapsed downward. Ely pushed aside the boards that cracked and clattered as they fell. At last the trio emerged out the back of the burned-out ruins. A steep precipice ran along the back of the destroyed buildings, but there was just enough space for a path behind them to the center of town.

The rage of the beast resounded once more, its deafening roar causing pain in Ellis's head. At the northern end of the charred buildings, a wall suddenly collapsed, crashing to the ground.

"It's here!" Alicia breathed.

Ely pulled Ellis to the ground, setting her with her back against the rear wall of what once had been a flower shop.

Alicia scrambled quickly to sit next to her with Ely on the other side.

"It was southeast of town," Alicia whispered hoarsely.

"What?" Ellis was not sure she had heard the young woman properly.

"The gate was southeast of town," Alicia said with urgency. "It isn't there anymore—or it wasn't when I last went looking for it—but that's where you found it when you left. On the far side of a field, down a narrow path through the trees there's a small church."

The memory came unbidden into Ellis's mind. *The Children's Church. She had never seen it before. It was so bright and the gate was open. . . .*

"How do you know this?" Ellis demanded.

"Because . . . because I was there, Ellis," Alicia said, tears streaking the soot on her face. "I'm the one that brought Jenny back. I was there when you left. I hoped you would never come back. Hoped you would go away and never be seen among us again."

"Where did I go, Alicia?" Ellis asked quietly.

Alicia turned her face to Ellis, her large eyes shining in the moonlight, her face stained and filthy. "Mortality."

"Get ready!" Ely muttered under his breath, pulling his feet under him and rising to a crouch. "We've got to get down to the end of these buildings and cross the street past the church!"

Ellis struggled to her feet, following Ely along the back of the ruins. She glanced back at the young woman behind her. "Come on, Alicia. It's not far."

"Go home, Ellis." Alicia stood still, her party dress torn

and soot stained. She flashed a sad smile at Ellis. "You're terrible at this game. It won't hurt me . . . I *know* what it wants!"

"Alicia!" Ellis called out as loudly as she dared. "No!"

"Don't get caught, Ellis." Alicia laughed as she ran, a giggling, hideous cackle of hysteria. She skipped along behind the burned-out shells of the southern shops and turned the corner toward the street, vanishing from sight.

Alicia's cackle became a terrified scream as the shadow of the beast cast itself over the ruins where she ran. The screams echoed on and on through the streets as the unseen creature snarled. Unspeakable rending sounds like the tearing of wet cloth merged with the shrieks.

"Run!" Ely shouted. "Run now!"

Ellis gathered up her skirts and ran after Ely. The horrible sounds followed them, fading slightly with every rushed footfall. They came to Sycamore Street. Ellis could see the park on the far side of the road with the burned-out shell of the church beyond.

"Keep running," Ely urged. "Don't look back!"

Ellis followed at a run in Ely's footsteps, crossing Elm and plunging headlong into the park. The screams and the rending sounds had stopped, but the howling had continued. She could feel her party shoes slipping on the wet grass as she rushed up the incline of the park. The blackened pews were achingly close, each facing the exposed lectern at the southernmost end. Ely was running faster than she could keep up, heading toward the southern corner of the gutted structure.

"This way!" called a hoarse voice. "Quick now!"

Ellis saw Ely hesitate and then dash directly toward the

church. She followed Ely's course, the howling behind her increasing with every step. As she passed the farthest trees she saw it: the black abyss of an open door beckoning her into the basement of the badly damaged rectory at the back of the collapsed chapel.

It reminded her of an open grave, but the baying drove her forward and she plunged into the darkness.

A strong, rough hand caught her at the waist, a second clamped at once over her mouth.

"Quiet now, miss," came the whisper. "Be calm."

Thunderous footfalls pounded the ground around her. The burnt smell was overwhelming in the pitch-blackness. The beast moved somewhere in that darkness and all Ellis could do was tremble in the strong arms that held her. The deafening screams of the frustrated beast pierced her soul. Then there followed another terrible crash and the footfalls of the creature grew more faint.

Suddenly they vanished altogether.

Ellis shook violently in the strong grip but dared not struggle.

Ellis heard Ely whisper from the darkness to her right, "Do you think—"

"Quiet, lad," warned the man who held her from behind. "Not yet."

Ellis felt as though she could hardly breathe. The moments in the darkness stretched into an eternity before the rough voice behind her spoke again.

"I think that's enough now," the man said softly. "Ely, be a good lad. There's a hurricane lamp on the table just behind you and a box of matches as well. Give us a little light, will you now?"

"But that thing . . ." Ely protested.

"I've blanketed the windows, boy, and the door as well," the voice replied gruffly. "We're as safe as I can make us."

Ellis heard the fumbling in the darkness. The flare of the match strike was momentarily blinding. It subsided into a dim, warm glow. Ely's back took the shape of a silhouette in the darkness as the glimmer from the lantern in front of him strengthened and grew. She could see that they were in the shattered remains of the church basement. Thick blankets had been nailed up over the broken windows and at the edges of the door. Timbers had been set up to brace the ceiling and one sagging wall. There was a single salvaged pew at one side of the space and a pair of mismatched chairs. Several maps of Gamin and its environs were tacked to the scorched far wall.

The rough hands slowly released Ellis. She stepped away at once, turning to face the man with the sad eyes and the hound-dog face.

"This is Captain Isaiah Walker," Ely said as though he were introducing them at tea. "Captain, Miss Ellis Harkington."

"Miss Harkington." The captain took off his stocking cap and bowed awkwardly. "No need to worry here, ma'am. That thing don't much care for sniffing around the church—never has from what I hear. Not too fond of it myself, if you take my meaning. We've a little time, anyway, before it comes back."

"There's a problem, Captain," Ely said, placing his hands on his knees as he tried to catch his breath.

"Problem?" Walker said, turning to Ely. "You said she knew the gate, Ely?"

"No!" Ellis said, exasperated and confused.

Both men turned to her.

"No!" she repeated, tears filling her eyes. "I *don't* know anything! I don't know where I am, or who I am, or who you *think* I am or anything about this gate everyone keeps asking me about! *Where am I? What is this place?*"

"You haven't *told* her?" Walker said, turning his accusing eye back on the young man.

"You know the rules," Ely said, a whine creeping into his tone. "We've tried everything we could think of to help her—"

"You Gamin folk and your games! You wouldn't know truth if it bit you on the street," Walker snarled. He turned back to Ellis, gesturing toward one of the chairs. "Please sit down, miss. I need to tell you a little story and we don't have a lot of time for it."

Ellis considered protesting for a moment, but the truth was her legs felt uncertain under her. She reached for the back of the chair and lowered herself onto the cushion carefully.

Walker grabbed the wooden chair and set it a few feet in front of Ellis, its back toward her. He then sat on the chair, his legs straddling the back and his large arms resting on the top edge of the chair. "What's the first thing you remember, lass?"

Ellis hesitated. "I was on the train, coming into Gamin. Miss Disir—Finny Disir—was riding with me. There was a baby in a basket—"

The captain raised his thick eyebrows at this. "And what do you remember before that?"

"Well, nothing, really," Ellis said. "Nightmares, dreams, perhaps, but nothing more."

"No one dreams here, Miss Ellis," the captain said, shaking his head. "Those were memories, not dreams."

"What do they mean?" Ellis asked.

"Well, lass, maybe this little tale will help answer that. This story happened long before your little train ride," Walker began. "Before your nightmares and even before the day you were born into the world."

"Walker, don't," Ely said, fear evident in his voice. "You know it's against the rules . . . we're *never* to speak of it."

Walker swatted a hand in Ely's direction as though waving away a fly. "There was a time when all souls of heaven came together to consider the course they would chart for their mortal lives. The king called on two princes of heaven to map the way. But these two princes had different ideas about which course to take, see? One of them said, 'Let's get born into the mortal world, live out our days and do what we're told like the good seagoing hands we all want to be and once we've had our mortal time we'll all come back again and be none the wiser.' That seemed right fair to about a third of us; we put in our work and get our pay without having to bother about having any responsibility for ourselves. But there was this other prince who had a different course in mind: it were a stormy one with difficult seas and unseen breakers. That were because no one were there to tell us what course we should steer—we would have to captain our own souls through the

world of trouble and some of us would founder, but those
what found their way would be captains in their own right
and the stronger for it."

"That's . . . a fanciful story, Captain Walker," Ellis said,
voicing a calm that she did not feel.

"Oh, it be more than a story, ma'am," Walker said, resting his chin atop his hands on the chair's back as he spoke.
"You see, there was such disagreement about which of these
courses should be steered that there was a war between them
souls."

"A war in heaven," Ely added.

"Aye, a war in heaven," Walker continued. "And in this
war, these souls had to choose their side. Most went with the
second prince—"

"He was the first prince," Ely corrected.

"I'm telling the story!" Walker barked, then lowered his
voice to continue, "Most followed this second prince, confident they could navigate the difficult course. A third of us
followed the first prince hoping for an easier course to follow.
In the end, this second prince had defeated his brother. Them
what followed the first prince were cheated out of our turn
to walk the mortal world and only them of the second prince
were born and lived out their mortal lives."

Isaiah leaned forward on his chair, coming closer to Ellis.

"So these souls chose one side or the other—but not all,"
Walker said quietly. "Them that chose the first prince went
to hell. Them that chose the second prince went to heaven. But
there were *another* crew that neither of the princes had a place
for . . . them that decided *not to choose at all*."

"Decided not to choose?" Ellis shook her head. "That makes no sense!"

"Well, that depends upon your tack," Walker said, leaning back on his chair. "The gist of it was that they did not wish to choose at all. They wished to abstain from this war in heaven and chose neither prince one way or the other. There was no place in heaven for them, for they had not chosen heaven's course. There was no place in hell for them, either. Neither of the princes, under the law of the king, could claim them. So, can you guess what happened to these troublesome souls?"

Ellis closed her eyes.

Merrick smiled at her, his arm sweeping outward. She saw the town for the first time and was delighted. . . .

"They came here," Ellis murmured as she opened her eyes.

"Quite right." Walker smiled, but his eyes reflected a deep sadness. "To a place beyond heaven and beyond hell. To a place of the doubly damned—unfit for either."

"It's a prison then?" Ellis asked.

"No, folks leave here from time to time in various ways and for various reasons," Walker said. "But none of them ever left the way *you* did, Miss Ellis . . . and none of them *ever* came back."

"Back." Ellis nodded slowly. "Back from where?"

"Life," Walker said simply. "Back from mortality."

Ellis turned toward Ely. "Am I dead, then?"

"We don't know—maybe." Ely turned away from her as he spoke. "Or near death, perhaps. We don't really know enough about it to say. At least, if you *are* dead, you must have lived once, and that's a great deal more than any of us can say."

"All we really know is that you found a way out of Gamin and into the mortal world without having to submit either to heaven or hell," Walker said as he stood up. "That makes you our best hope of escaping Gamin. You found the gate once, Miss Ellis; you need to be finding it again."

"Alicia said I was somewhere south of town when I found this gate before—"

"It's not there anymore," Ely said, anxiety rising in his voice. "We've looked. Merrick must have moved it after you were gone."

"These fools have it all wrong, Miss Ellis," Walker said, his eyes glancing up at the sagging ceiling above them. "You don't have to *remember* where it was . . . you have to realize where it is now."

The fog rolled away, revealing the town far below them. "Name it," *Merrick said.* "Name our new home. . . ."

"We . . . we were ab-b-bove the town," Ellis stammered, struggling with the impressions that flashed through her mind. "It was my favorite place . . . our first place."

Ely looked up slowly. "Did you feel that?"

"Gamin," *she said as she looked down.* *"We'll call it Gamin."*

Merrick smiled at her. *"A fine joke indeed!"*

The captain ignored Ely, concentrating on Ellis. "What did you see there?"

"A bay in summer. There were little boats on the water down below us." Ellis smiled softly with the memory, but it faded into another thought. "No, another bay in winter. There were large ships: iron and rust and darkness."

"The mountain," Walker said. "The mountain to the northwest. That could be it. All we need to do is—"

The trumpeting roar of the beast blew apart the ceiling overhead. Ellis fell sideways out of her chair onto the floor. Ely and Walker both recoiled from the blast, their arms raised to shield them against the tumult of debris.

Ellis looked up and screamed.

A hole gaped overhead. Beyond it was a hoary, gigantic shape silhouetted against the moonlit clouds beyond. Its form was that of an enormous jackal, at least fifteen feet high to its muscular shoulders. Its wide grinning mouth was filled with gleaming teeth and its featureless eyes shone with unnatural light. Its ears lay flat against its wide head while impossible leathery wings, sprouting from between its shoulders, spread out to cover the clouds.

Worse, a dark paisley mark ran from around its eye and across its forehead.

Ely bolted for the door, but it was too late. The demonic jackal head struck with incredible speed down through the opening, its jaws clamping down mercilessly around the young man's body. Ely shrieked as the monster dragged him up through the hole in the ceiling, crushing his body with its powerful jaws. The monstrous head rose up high above the shattered church, then shook with such violent force that Ely's body tore between its teeth, snapping in two.

The body of Ely at once became a mass of moths. In moments his form had dissolved into a dissipating cloud of the insects, flitting off into the night.

Walker lunged for the door. "Come on, woman! Run!"

Ellis tried to get to her feet, but the monstrous jackal was already rushing down.

The ceiling collapsed down on top of her.

20

PREY

"Ellis! Wake up!"

Ellis took in a gasping breath; her eyes flew open. She had the panicked feeling she was falling. Her fingers curled around the bedcovers in a vise-like grip.

The common sight of her room was as much of a shock to her as the nightmare she had been living. She took in the cream-colored ceiling, the plaster ornamentation in the corners. Her chest of drawers stood in the corner. Evening light was dim through the French doors that led out to the small balcony. A gentle rain fell against the glass as the beam of Curtis Lighthouse swept past the glass doors. She struggled to sit up.

"Don't rouse yourself, dearie," Finny Disir said, pushing her back down into the comfortable folds of the sheets, blankets and coverlets. Finny was wearing her nurse's uniform again. Her eyes were cold as ice. "You've been through a terrible ordeal, but the fever broke and the worst is over now."

"What are you talking about?" Ellis shivered despite the layers of blanket pressing down on her. "What are you doing here?"

"I'm your nurse, Miss Harkington," Finny sniffed as she straightened up by the side of the bed. She obviously considered Ellis's question to be impertinent. "Just relax. There's no sense in making yourself upset. You've been delirious for several days now. You've given us quite a scare, young woman."

"I've given *you* a scare?" Ellis asked.

A tall man inexplicably dressed in a gray morning suit and cloak threw open the door to her bedroom and stepped purposefully toward the startled Ellis. Rainwater dripped to the floor from his coat, his hair wet.

"Mr. Bacchus!" Ellis exclaimed, dragging the bedclothes up to her chin.

Merrick took no notice of her discomfiture but spoke briskly to the nurse and he removed his cloak, tossing it over the chair in the corner of the room. "Miss Disir, you will go at once and prepare some tea. I need to speak with Miss Harkington for a moment."

Finny sputtered, "But Mr. Bacchus, sir—"

"At once, Nurse Disir," Merrick insisted. "I've not the time or the patience for questions at the moment."

Finny lifted her pinched face in disapproval but stepped from the room, leaving them entirely alone.

Merrick turned and sat on the edge of Ellis's bed. The young woman withdrew from him as best she could, uncomfortably aware of how narrow the bed now seemed and how close this man was to her. It was a gesture of intimacy for which she was not prepared: a return to the nightmare.

Merrick cocked his head, listening for Finny's steps on the stairs to fade away before he turned back to Ellis. His eyes were filled with sadness and concern. "I got word that you had emerged from your fevered delirium this morning and came as quickly as I could. I've been worried to distraction for you ever since this whole thing happened. How are you feeling this morning?"

"I . . . I'm not certain," Ellis answered. "Tired, I think, and confused."

"I understand from Dr. Carmichael that it is not unusual in cases like yours." Merrick nodded. He reached out from where he sat, gently resting his hand on the coverlet over her leg. Ellis jerked both her legs abruptly back toward her chin, glaring a fearful warning at Merrick. He sighed, pulling his hand back reluctantly. "He also said it would take some time before you would be back to your old self. Nurse Disir is here to help you, Ellis, but I'm afraid I have to ask you a few questions."

"Questions?" Ellis glared at Merrick. "What questions?"

"Well, they are not *my* questions," Merrick pressed on. "The constable needs some information if we're to find the monster that did this to you, Ellis. I know it may be hard for you, but you have to be brave."

"I've a few questions of my own," Ellis insisted. "What *did* happen to me?"

"You witnessed a murder, Ellis," Merrick said. He turned

to look out over the bay toward the lighthouse. "A horrific, terrible murder perpetrated by a monster. There have been a series of them that have followed you all the way down the coast from Halifax—"

"I came from Halifax?" Ellis asked suddenly. It was the first time she could recall anyone volunteering some truth they knew about her.

"Yes," Merrick said through a soft smile. "That's where you came from, Ellis—your other home. You arrived here last Sunday with your friend, Miss Cochrane."

"No, that's not true," Ellis said, her lip quivering. "I don't know anyone by the name of Cochrane. I've been here for weeks now—"

"You've been here for five days," Merrick asserted.

Ellis swallowed this news mutely, trying to believe him, wanting to scream that he was wrong. She asked her next question hoping for an answer she could believe.

"Why was I sent here?"

"You were sent here to get away from this creature," Merrick said, looking away. "This monster appears to be masquerading as a man—an outsider. He may be someone you knew in Halifax and it appears that he has been leaving a trail of horror as he has stalked you here to Gamin. His latest victim was Miss Cochrane . . . that artist you had invited to stay with you here. Three days ago we discovered what remained of her out by the point. Dr. Carmichael believes you were there, saw the gruesome attack and somehow escaped the fiend who had grimly assaulted your friend. He also believes you may have witnessed the other attacks before that as well.

We found you that same day wandering along the beach below Summersend, your clothing shredded. You were raving madness—"

"What do you mean?" Ellis insisted.

"Something about arriving on a train . . . a baby . . . something called a 'Nightbird,'" Merrick said, shaking his head. "Nurse Disir took most of it down at the insistence of the doctor. But part of your delirium was a dark figure of a man who came to you here in your room. Do you remember him?"

A male form became clearly outlined, darkness against the moonlight now streaming through the window at his back. His silhouette was tall, with broad shoulders and slender hips. The ribbons upon his chest glistened in the moonlight, head bent low, face hidden in the shadows.

"A soldier," Ellis said quietly.

"Ah!" Merrick urged as he nodded. "That's helpful. Did you know him?"

"Dear Ellis." He sighed. "Do you know me?" She could see the set of his jawline was earnest in the darkness. Almost imperceptibly she shook her head no.

"He thought I did," Ellis replied, licking her lips.

"Did he have a name?" Merrick pressed her. "Do you remember if he gave you his name?"

The waltz started playing on the Victrola.

Transfixed, Ellis spun with him into the small world of their dance.

"Do you know me?" he asked with hope.

Passion. Heat. Pain. Desire. Giving. Taking. Holding. Fear. His voice called up thoughts and impressions unbidden. Terrible. Familiar.

"Who are you?" Ellis gasped as all of Gamin whirled around them.

"I am Jonas," he said.

Ecstasy. Trembling. Anger. Betrayal. Tears.

"I don't know you." She knew it was a lie even as she spoke the words.

"He did." Ellis sighed. "He said his name was Jonas."

"That's excellent, Ellis." Merrick nodded. "Did he ever call himself by any other name or—"

Ellis shook her head. "No more, please. I'm tired. I've got to rest."

"Of course, Ellie," Merrick said. He hesitated, looking away from her again through the French doors to the failing light beyond. He winced every time the beam of the lighthouse crossed his face. "I don't know what happened to us, Ellis. We were happy here, you and I—as happy as two souls might be here in Gamin. You loved this place. You used to say that you came here just because I asked. It was enough for you—enough for us. I could not understand it when you left. I would have come after you if I could have. Then you came back and I was sure that we could fix whatever had gone wrong between us and we could continue on as though nothing had changed."

"I don't remember any of that," Ellis said. She could see the pain in his eyes, the defiance against his own emotions in the jutting of his jaw. "I wish I could."

"So do I," Merrick said through a sad smile, and then rose from the edge of the bed. He leaned forward carefully, hesitantly, and then kissed her gently on her forehead. He lingered there close to her for a moment, murmuring quietly, "We were always good together . . . and we will be again."

"You should go," Ellis answered back.

"Quite right," Merrick said, straightening upright at once and stepping away from the bed. "The constable is awaiting my report and then I have a number of other important things which demand my immediate attention."

Merrick snatched up his cloak from the chair, swinging it onto his shoulders. "We'll have this fiend cornered and caged by morning. You've come back to us and are safely home at last. That's all that matters. The nightmare is nearly over, Janelle."

Ellis glanced up sharply. "What did you call me?"

"Ellie, of course," Merrick replied with concern. "Are you feeling unwell again?"

"Thank you for your concern, but—"

Merrick opened the door, calling down the spiral staircase, "Nurse Disir!"

"Yes, sir?" came the distant voice from below.

"Attend to Miss Harkington at once," Merrick demanded, then turned back to face Ellis from the doorway as he fastened his cloak. "Just stay here in your rooms until I return and you'll be safe."

"Yes, Merrick," Ellis replied.

He smiled. "That's the first time you've called me by that name. Thank you, Ellie."

Bacchus pushed past Finny on the landing. His footfalls

vanished down the curved staircase into the rotunda below as Finny regained control of the precariously balanced tea tray in her hands.

"That Mr. Bacchus is always in too much of a hurry!" Finny exclaimed as she came into the room, her face as sour as the lemon slices on the tray. "Haste is blind and improvident, that is what I always say. I've brought you up the tea, miss."

"Thank you, Finny," Ellis said, pushing her feet back down the length of the bed under the covers. She helped Finny position the bed tray over her lap. "Where's Jenny? I would have thought she would have been asking after me by now."

"Jenny, miss?" Finny asked evenly as she picked up the teapot.

"Yes, Jenny." Ellis asked, "Where is she?"

"I don't know any Jenny, miss," Finny answered as she carefully poured out the tea into its cup. Would you care for any cream?"

"Yes, thank you. Of course you know Jenny. She's the young woman who lives here," Ellis insisted. "The one who owns Summersend."

"Oh, I think you're still feeling a bit confused," Finny said as the cream began to cloud the surface of the clear tea. "You're the only mistress of Summersend and have been these last six years since your parents passed on."

Ellis stared at Finny for a moment. She drew in a deep, considering breath before she spoke. "Oh, of course, how silly of me. I must be confusing my nightmares with my waking hours."

"Yes, miss." Finny nodded with a tight smile. "Sugar?"

"Yes, thank you," Ellis said, her voice as cool as the rain splattering the window. The beam of the lighthouse passed again, somehow brighter in the deepening evening. She fixed her eyes on the nurse fumbling with the spoon over the sugar bowl. "I had a rather fanciful dream about a sea captain . . . a Captain Walker. Have you ever heard of such a man?"

"Oh no, miss," Finny said, her hand shaking as she sifted the sugar into the cup.

"There were also a young man and a young woman in this dream," Ellis continued. "His name was Ely Rossini. I called the woman Alicia."

"I'm not in the habit of dealing with fictitious individuals," Finny said, straightening up.

"So, you've never known someone named Alicia?" Ellis asked as she picked up the cup.

"Stuff and nonsense!" Finny sniffed in disgust. "I'm a serious-minded woman, miss, and I've no interest in being introduced to your imaginary friends called into existence by a fevered mind!"

"No, of course not." Ellis nodded, her eyes fixed on Finny over the edge of the cup as she sipped her tea. "I guess I'm still on the mend."

"Of course, miss." Finny nodded, her arms folded across her chest, fingers drumming in her impatience. "Will there be anything else? The weather is getting worse and I'd like to be home before the light fails entirely."

"No, that will be all—"

Finny nodded and was already turning.

"No, wait," Ellis added. "There is one last thing you can do for me before you go."

Finny turned, casting a baleful eye on Ellis as she asked, "And what would that be, miss?"

"Is there a bell jar in the hall downstairs?" Ellis asked with a gentle smile, her head cocked slightly to one side.

"The large one?" Finny asked. "The one displaying all those dead moths?"

"The very one." Ellis nodded. "Would you bring it up and set it on my dresser? I'm tired of staring at the walls and long to see it."

Finny opened her mouth but paused before she spoke. "Yes, miss."

The nurse left the room for a few moments and then returned with the large bell jar carried awkwardly in front of her. The glass rattled on the base as she lifted it up onto the top of the dresser. At last she managed to slide it back into the center of the dresser's top, stepped back and straightened her dress before turning to face Ellis again.

"Miss, I don't think—"

"That will be all, Finny," Ellis said, sipping her tea once more. "You should be off home while you can."

"Yes, miss," Finny said as she retreated quickly from the room. "I'll be back in the morning. Night, miss."

Ellis waited, patiently sipping her tea until she heard the

footsteps downstairs end with the closing of the front door. Then she set down the cup, picked up the tray and kicked off the covers. She set the tray carefully on the floor, hurrying over to the dresser, inspecting the interior of the bell jar carefully.

The vertical piece of driftwood in the center with the various leaves and mosses fixed to it was as she remembered it. The wings of the moths were carefully arranged into a beautiful presentation, but now the display had changed. Two more moths had been added.

"Ely and Alicia," Ellis murmured.

The wings of the two new dead moths twitched slightly in the bright passing beam of the lighthouse.

"I'm not mad," Ellis said as she stepped back. "The world is."

She opened the closet cabinet, scanning its contents. She pulled out the dark green skirt and jacket of her traveling outfit. She frowned; it was still ugly in her eyes, but suddenly she felt as though it was the only thing among her clothes that was truly hers. She pulled out the rest of her traveling suit and quickly dressed, finishing with the buttons of her high kid boots.

She looked at herself in the mirror and adjudged herself as ready as she could be.

"You seem to be the only one here that knows what's going on," she said to her reflection, "and you don't know a blessed thing. The only thing you *do* know is that no one is going to stop this except you."

She turned to the French doors, released the latches and

pulled them open wide. The light rain fell on the small balcony beyond. Through the veil of rain she barely made out
the lighthouse. Its beam swung over her.

"You want me, Jonas!" she called into the rain. "I'm here!
Come and get me!"

21

SNARES

The beam of the lighthouse swung around with clock-work regularity, cutting through the sheets of light rain over the harbor. Ellis waited, staring out toward Curtis Island with calm anticipation. She was tired of wondering, tired of feeling lost, tired of questioning her own mind and fleeing from fear. She stood facing the light. She was suddenly aware of how much her traveling suit looked like a uniform and she felt somehow that she was about to engage in her own private war.

They had told her she was sick and, believing them, she had been weak. They had told her she was mad and, believing them, she had accepted their madness.

But she no longer believed them.

She was strong.

She was sane.

And she could fight her monsters on her own.

The light swung again toward her, filling her vision as she stared toward it. But the brilliance did not fade as it had countless times before. It cut through the rain. The light remained constant across the threshold of the French doors, spilling across the small balcony and filling her room. Ellis held her hand up, shielding her eyes against the blinding light. Whether the lamp had stopped or time itself Ellis could not tell.

Something moved in the brilliance. Shadows incongruously fluttered away from the light, a thousand shades of darkness in paisley shapes flying toward her. Ellis took a single step back, then steeled herself for what she both hoped and feared was coming.

The moths exploded into the room around her, a whirl-wind of dark wings. Ellis balled up her fists, holding still against the frightening onslaught. The cloud of moths around her suddenly collapsed into the shape of a man in front of her.

Time resumed and the beam of the lighthouse passed on.

Jonas stood before her, the distinctive paisley-shaped discoloration blemishing the skin of his forehead and right eye. He stood in his soldier's uniform—not a dress uniform but that of an infantryman in Europe as she had seen them pictured.

Ellis forced a smile to her lips.

"I came, Ellis," Jonas said, taking her in his arms boldly, passionate with a warm familiarity that both shocked and comforted Ellis all at once. "You called me at last and I've come for you."

"Yes, Jonas," Ellis said with a lightness she did not feel. "You've come as I asked."

"Come with me, Ellis," Jonas said. "We must leave soon. So much depends on it—more than you know."

"Go where, Jonas?" Ellis urged.

"To the gate, my darling," Jonas said. "Once we pass through the gate everything will be right again."

"The gate out of this world?" Ellis asked carefully.

"The gate into the next," Jonas replied.

"Then we must hurry before they discover us." Ellis nodded. "Come, Jonas; I know the way."

Ellis took Jonas by the hand and led him from the room. From the landing at the top of the stairs the floor of the rotunda was dim under the light of the evening storm. They walked down the stairs carefully into the darkness below them.

"Where is the gate, Ellie?" Jonas asked.

"It took me a while before I realized it," Ellis replied. "Ely told me that Merrick moved the gate after I left, but it wasn't until today that I realized just where he would have thought to move it."

They came to the parquet floor with the inlaid compass design barely visible in the failing light. Ellis walked down the vestibule and into the dim music room with Jonas following close behind. She noted that the piano was gone entirely; a pair of high-back chairs with a small, round table between them had taken its place. She dismissed the mystery to the madness of the world, concentrating on leading Jonas on behind her. She stepped up to the bookcase at the back and found the vase on the shelf. Ellis pulled open the hidden door in the bookcase and beckoned Jonas to follow her.

"A secret room?" Jonas was surprised.

"Very secret indeed," Ellis responded. "Where better to keep secrets?"

Ellis picked up the vase as she stepped into the workroom, holding the door open for Jonas as he followed.

"The gate is here?" Jonas asked.

"There, toward the far end," Ellis said as she set the vase down on the workbench. "Beneath the window there's a catch."

Jonas stepped down to the far end of the room. "I can't see it. It's too dark in here."

"I'll fetch a lamp," Ellis said easily.

She turned and pushed against the second hidden door.

It did not move.

Ellis's hands began to shake, but she pushed again.

This time the panel gave way, swinging open into the archway at the back of the rotunda. Ellis stepped through it, her hand reaching up for the second vase.

He's a monster, Ellis reminded herself. *He's killed before . . . maybe he's killed Jenny. He has affected the minds of everyone in the town. It's up to me. I have to put an end to this.*

Ellis pulled the vase from the bookcase in the archway. The hidden door swung quietly closed as she stepped clear. She heard the lock click shut with a dull thunk.

Ellis had trapped the monster, but she did not know for how long.

She fled from the house into the rain.

.   .   .

Her shoes were soaked and caked with mud. The hem of her skirt was stained and her jacket drenched with the rain. Her hair had become soaked as she ran and lay in short, wet tendrils about her head and face as she staggered up the steps of the Norembega. She pushed open the vestibule outer doors. She eyed the cord for the bell next to the inner door but laughed at the thought of waiting on custom at this moment of peril. She reached for the door latch and was surprised to find the door unsecured. It swung open in front of her.

"Mr. Bacchus!" she yelled. "Please! Merrick!"

She closed the door behind her, throwing home the bolt, and then staggered back away from the door. The oak stairs with their sitting-room landing were there as she remembered them on her right and the large front parlor through the doors to her left. There was a small fire burning in the fireplace at the far end of the parlor with the archway to the half-round office room just to its right. The rain pelted the high windows of the curved room beyond as well as the windows in their bays on the right side of the room. There were other doors leading in several other directions from the hall and on the left side of the parlor, but she hesitated to go through them. Ellis had not ventured farther into the house than this on her visit and suddenly realized that she would have no idea where to look for Merrick in the enormous mansion.

"Merrick!" Ellis screamed. "Help! Where are you? I need you!"

She stumbled wearily into the parlor. The statues of griffins on either side of the hearth seemed to watch her as she approached. She could see the glass bowl still on the mantelpiece, its silver key obscured by the etched surface. She slipped past the fireplace into the turret room beyond.

Much to her surprise, the desk that had previously occupied the space behind the fireplace was missing, as was its chair. Only the wooden books remained, filling the bookshelves with empty knowledge.

Ellis ran her fingers through her hair over her forehead, trying to think. Merrick said he had things to which he had to attend. Perhaps he was caught somewhere else when the rain came down in earnest. She gazed out the windows set high in the curved wall, her breath still labored from her flight from the house.

Across the south lawn she saw it.

There was a light flickering in the carriage house.

Merrick!

Ellis considered for a moment. Merrick had forbidden anyone to go into the carriage house. Perhaps it was his private retreat, a place where he could get away from the prying eyes and the wagging tongues of the town. A man of his position surely needed some place that was inviolate.

Surely, however, he would make an exception for this . . . for her.

Ellis hurried back into the parlor, quickly snatching the key from the bowl on the mantel.

Surely, he would make an exception. . . .

.   .   .

Ellis looked up at the carriage house, the rain washing down over her face. A spindly narrow turret rose above her, capped by a slate cone and a widow's walk around its crest. The main doors of the carriage house rose before her, light spilling out from beneath the doors.

Ellis stepped up to the door, intent on putting the key in the padlock, but discovered that it was hanging open. She slipped the key into her jacket pocket, swung the latch to the side and opened the door just enough to slip into the space beyond.

It was difficult for Ellis to see the extent of the large open space. The light was coming from an open trapdoor in the floor at the far end of the carriage stalls that ran nearly the length of the structure. Light glimmered off the finish of a pair of carriages, but Merrick's automobile was not here.

"Merrick?" Ellis called out toward the lit patch in the floor.

She plunged through the dark space toward the light.

A ladder led down through the trapdoor to the storage space beneath.

"Merrick!" Ellis called out. "Please, I need your help!"

Frustrated at receiving no answer, Ellis slipped quickly down the ladder.

The wooden walls were unfinished and rough. The room was wide though not as wide as the carriage space above and felt cramped. There was a hallway with a series of closed doors on either side that ran down into the darkness beyond.

In the center of the room, however, was the desk from Merrick's study, gleaming beneath the light of a well-trimmed

lamp. His chair was set behind it as though he had only re-
cently abandoned it. There was an ink and quill set as well as
a number of pencils.

All of these were set around a pale green book with an
embossed cover.

He must have only just left, Ellis thought as she stepped
around the desk. *He'll be back in a moment and find me.*

The writing on the cover of the book caught her eye.

Gamin.

Merrick's scrapbook? Ellis's brow furrowed. *Jenny said that
they all kept them, but Merrick hardly seems like the type that would
gather scraps of anything.*

She reached out for the book and turned open the cover.
She took in a startled breath.

A crude sketch of her face stared back at her. Beneath it
was written: "The Book of Our Day."

Ellis began turning the pages. Most were filled with notations and terribly small writing that was difficult to read in
the lamplight. Some of the larger notations, however, she
could read.

Rules of the Day . . .
Outsiders . . .
Gamin . . .
Soldiers . . .
Demons . . .

All of these writings, however, were surrounding sketches
and scraps cut from pictures. Here was the Norembega drawn

in careful detail although the proportions were strangely off, drawings of Summersend, the Nightbirds Literary Society House and other places in the town.

She caught her breath.

A sketch of a gate.

"Alicia! Come on; I think I can see something on the other side!"

"No! You know it is against the Rules of the Day!" Alicia said. *"He'll be angrier with you than he is already! Let's go back!"*

"But we found the gate! Doesn't that mean we win? We could have our very own day!"

Ellis's hand began to shake. She turned another page.

The writing grew more chopped and less precise. There was anger in the writing that grew with each turn of the page.

The sketches continued to illuminate the pages. A sketch of Jenny with her crippled hand. A sketch of Gamin in flames. Dr. Carmichael . . . Captain Walker . . . shipwrecks . . . soldiers . . . the burnt church . . .

Then a sketch of the interior of a Pullman car, with Ellis in her ugly green traveling dress, Finny Disir in her nurse's uniform. More writing here, written with a hasty hand, as Ellis turned the page again.

Erasures. A rough sketch of Ely nearly obliterated. The artist from the station scratched out. A picture of Alicia with the head torn from the page. A picture of the key in Ellis's pocket with dark liquid drawn dripping from it.

Trembling, Ellis turned another page.

A monster sketched in pencil. The head of a jackal and large, leathery wings sprouting from its back.

Carefully rendered on the jackal face was a great paisley mark.

Ellis was startled by a noise behind her.

Something shifted behind the first door in the long hall.

Ellis closed the book carefully, then picked up the lamp from the desk. She walked with quiet, careful steps toward the door.

"Merrick?" she called out softly. "Is that you?"

The door was secured by a silver lock set into the door just below the knob.

Ellis paused, then reached into the pocket of her jacket. She produced the silver key. It looked clean and bright. She slipped it expectantly into the lock.

It fit perfectly. She felt the bolt slide easily as she turned the key. Gripping the knob with her free hand, she turned it and pulled open the door, holding the lantern high as she stared into the room beyond.

The dead eyes of Alicia Van der Meer stared back at her.

22

BLEEDING KEYS

Ellis took several steps back, pulling the lamp away from the open door and allowing the darkness to shadow the awful display within.

It was not just the body of Alicia that was found within the closeted space. Her body lay at the foremost edge of a stack of other bodies piled inside one on top of the other and pushed toward the back of the cell. The dead were piled nearly to the rafters.

Ellis took a step forward, raising the lamp once more. Alicia, Ely, Isaiah, Martha, Silenus and a host of others lay within the space. The barber who had cut Jenny's hair. The members of the literary society. Jenny was not among them. Merrick had told Ellis that these people didn't exist, and now they did not. Curious, cold detachment settled over Ellis. *Alicia's neck shows the signs of deep puncture wounds, as does her right shoulder where the neckline of her dress slipped down. The dress is heavily stained, but the neck wounds, deep and extensive as they are, show no signs of bleeding. The shoulder wound exposes the bone and yet is similarly clean.*

Ellis was horrified and yet some inner part of her curiosity drove her forward. She leaned into the space, holding the lamp high with her left hand and reaching out with her right. She lifted Alicia's right arm up, examining it carefully.

Pallor mortis, Ellis thought as she looked under the arm and then dropped it carefully back into place. She looked down behind Alicia's neck. *Livor mortis but no rigor mortis. Blood pooling but no evidence of bleeding. Ely looks to be in a similar state. The artist girl shows no signs of putrification despite being dead far longer than either Alicia or Ely.*

Ellis leaned in closer still.

The artist girl shows cut marks consistent with the described dismemberment and yet her body appears to be intact, with none of the decomposition that was previously described. There's no distinctive odor, either, all of which is impossible given the time that had passed since the demise of some of the bodies. It is as if they were dolls, made of flesh and bone, whose strings had been cut—

Ellis suddenly stood up, appalled as much at her own actions as at the horrific scene before her. Wondering how she knew so much about the human body and could so calmly observe such gore, she stumbled back out of the room. Ellis turned hesitantly, looking down the hallway to her left . . . down the many doors lining the hall . . . doors exactly like the one she had just opened.

The sketched monster in Merrick's book . . . the bodies in Merrick's cellar . . .

Ellis felt sick in her realization.

I've trapped the wrong monster.

Ellis slammed the door shut, suppressing the scream that she felt rising within her. *Merrick told me never to come in here. He must not know that I've seen this. If he knows that I know . . .*

She reached into the jacket pocket, her shaking hands fumbling for the key.

He cannot know that I've see this. . . .

She finally grasped the cold of the silver key and pulled it out of her pocket. Ellis willed her hand to hold still as she struggled to insert the key back into the lock beneath the doorknob, dreading what she knew was beyond the closed door. The key at last slipped into the lock.

Ellis tried to turn the key, but her fingers slipped around its head suddenly warm and slick to her touch. Ellis reached for the key once more and gasped.

A crimson, viscous liquid dripped out of the keyhole, coating the key before it dripped down onto the floor in front of the door.

Blood flowed from the lock.

Ellis's breath quickened. She knew she had to get the key back into the bowl over the mantel of the house. If Merrick discovered it was missing . . .

She reached again for the key, gripping it tightly, her fingers pressing the warm gore away from the key to fall into the growing pool on the floor. The key turned with effort, pushing the bolt closed and locking the door once more. Ellis held the key as tightly as she could and pulled. The blade slid free of the lock with more ease than she expected.

Warmth ran down her hand.

It was not the lock that had been bleeding; it was the *key*. Blood flowed down between her fingers, following the curve of her wrist before it fell, spattering down the front of her green jacket and onto her skirt.

"No!" Ellis screamed. She dropped the lamp on the table and rushed up the ladder, vivid red stains blossoming on every rung. She dared not drop the key—Merrick would know that she had taken it. She needed to get the key back into the bowl, out of her hands, and get back to Summersend. Perhaps she could change then, wash away the stains, and Merrick would be none the wiser.

She fled from the carriage house, grateful to be back in the rain. The precipitation ran gratefully over her, a cleansing that she desperately desired. The blood still flowed from the key but was diluted as she ran across the hill back toward the house.

She stumbled into the vestibule at the front of the mansion and pushed open the heavy front door, heedless of the water cascading off of her clothing onto the polished wooden floor of the Norembega's front hall. The parlor was just to her right. She stepped into it, the key cupped in her hand as she moved toward the fireplace and the cut-glass bowl resting in the center of its mantel. She lifted her arms.

The twin griffin statues supporting the mantel shifted on the hearth, their heads turning toward Ellis.

Ellis skidded slightly on the polished wooden floor, trying desperately to stop. The griffin statues on either side of the firebox snapped out at her, their stone beaks clacking. Their feet and wings remained fixed to the hearth and firebox, but their necks and beaks craned forward, shifting and bobbing in snake-like movements as they lashed out at her. Ellis tried to reach the key over them to drop it into the glass bowl. The left griffin struck upward, the tip of its beak catching the jacket cloth of Ellis's outstretched arm, rending the sleeve at once and cutting into her forearm. She snatched her hand back with a cry.

The key continued to bleed, its crimson flowing down her torn sleeve, mixing with her own blood from her wound. She took a step back from the fireplace, searching the room for anything she might use to lift the key up over the animated statues and replace the key before she was discovered.

The griffins abruptly returned to their places—silent and unmoving.

Ellis watched them for a moment, then hesitantly took a step toward them, the key held in front of her, her eyes fixed on the bowl on the mantel.

"Ellis?"

She caught her breath. Ellis turned slowly, shifting her hands behind her with as casual a motion as she could manage, hiding the key behind her.

"What are you doing here?" Merrick stood in the archway of the entry. He was still wearing his morning coat and suit, but the cloak was drenched, as were the legs of his trousers. His eyes were fixed on Ellis, curious with a hint of sadness about them. "I told you to stay home."

"I couldn't," Ellis said. "I was . . . I was afraid."

"Afraid?" Merrick scoffed. He set the umbrella in a stand

next to the front door and began removing his cloak. "There's nothing to fear at Summersend, Ellis. It's the safest place in all of Gamin. I've seen to that."

"You are right, of course." Ellis nodded. Behind her was the curved study room in the turret. She knew there was no exit there. There was a sitting room to her right, but the doors were closed; she did not dare risk passing the fireplace or its griffins again to reach the room. The only other exit from this room was past where Merrick stood. "It was just a foolish panic of mine. I'm feeling much better now. I'll go home."

"In this weather?" Merrick chuckled.

"Well, as you can see, a little more rain could hardly matter now," Ellis said with a shrug and a smile. She started toward the entrance archway as if to pass Merrick. "I know you're busy."

Merrick's smile turned to a thoughtful expression as he stepped into Ellis's path, blocking her way. "Your dress is stained."

"Oh yes." Ellis nodded, though she did not dare look up into his face. "A little accident in the kitchen before I came. I don't know if I'll ever be able to get it out."

"You're bleeding," Merrick observed quietly. "It's pooling on the floor behind you."

"Oh yes." Ellis nodded. "I'm so sorry. That was the accident in the kitchen. Cut my arm. I panicked, I guess, and ran here before I properly dressed it. I'm feeling better now, though. I'll just hurry home and—"

Merrick shifted in front of her as she tried to step around him again. He gazed down at her, a slight curl to his lips.

"What do you have in your hand, Ellis?"

"Nothing," Ellis lied, taking a step back.

Merrick moved with her, standing uncomfortably close as he looked down at her. "Show me."

"Merrick, I really must—"

"*Show me!*" he demanded into her face with unbridled rage.

"I . . . I found this key, is all," Ellis said, her voice sounding small in her ears. "It's really nothing."

"You just couldn't leave it alone, could you?" Merrick's voice shook with quiet, barely controlled rage. "You had to ruin the game . . . and now you must pay the price."

His hands swung suddenly upward, gripping her by the lapels of her ruined jacket. He lifted her up off the ground with unexpected strength. Ellis tore at his hands with her fingernails, rending the backs of them, but his eyes remained cold and fixed on her, focused in their malice. He threw his head back, roaring with a trumpeting sound that was deafening. He threw her down the length of the parlor. Ellis tumbled across the polished wood, the key falling from her hand as she skittered to a stop near the archway to the study.

She drew herself up, trying to stand and face Merrick, but he was already coming for her.

"This is *my* day." Merrick seethed with each considered step. "I make the rules. I decide what is real and what is not. I did this all for us, Ellis, and then you had to spoil it! You wanted the day all for yourself! You couldn't trap me, so you had to leave me here!"

"Trap you?" Ellis snapped as she regained her footing.

Suddenly she realized what he was saying. "The workroom in Summersend! Jenny said I designed it. I created it for *you*, didn't I?"

"But it didn't do you any good, did it?" Merrick said.

"So now you're going to kill me," Ellis said, stepping away from him, her back against the bookshelves, knowing she had nowhere left to go. "Just as you killed all the others?"

"Oh, they aren't *dead*." Merrick grinned. "Not *that* way. This is worse . . . much worse, I hear."

"What have you done to them?" Ellis demanded.

"I've sent them away."

"Where?"

"To the Umbra, Ellis." Merrick chuckled. "To the place farthest from the light. Where everyone goes who breaks the rules of my day . . . and, Ellis, of all souls, how could you have broken the rules to my day? You have to go now, too, Ellis. You broke the rules of my day and I have to send you away."

"Then please," Ellis begged. She needed time to think, find something to defend herself. "Let me say my prayers . . . let me make my peace before you take my life."

"Prayers?" Merrick gave a hideous laugh, continuing toward her, passing through the arch into the half circle of the library. "Here? Just where do you think you are, Ellis, that prayer would be of any use at all?"

Rage played across Merrick's face, barely checked.

"It's time to visit the carriage house."

He reached down for her.

The glass of the library windows exploded inward, showering the room with shards as a wall of countless moths dove down around Ellis, shielding her in a chaotic whirlwind of beating wings. Through the sudden flurry of insects Ellis saw Merrick raise his hands against the razor-sharp slivers, several of which impaled his palms. Again he let out a trumpeting roar of outrage as the glass fell to the floor in a shower around him. He flew backward through the arch as though driven by a terrible wind, alighting on the floor in a crouch beneath the arch that led to the entryway.

Ellis felt the whirlwind of moths constricting around her, a stifling shroud. She pushed through the vortex, the hard soles of her shoes crunching across the shattered glass covering the floor between the library and the parlor. She turned before the fireplace toward the closed pocket doors to the music room, but the doors were locked shut, leaving her only avenue of escape through the entry and the door to the vestibule beyond.

Merrick stood slowly, barely contained rage causing the muscles in his face to twitch.

The vortex of moths coalesced, taking shape and substance. The shadows became a man resolving into one in a soldier's combat uniform, his hair in dark waves atop his head.

"I'm taking her with me," Jonas said, stepping forward to shield Ellis.

"You said that once before," Merrick snarled as he pulled several large glass shards out of his palm with his teeth and spat them to the ground. "And yet she came back here. I wonder which one of us she really wants to follow?"

Ellis, her back pressed against the barred pocket doors, stood between them.

23

DOORS

Jonas stood in the archway between the library's shattered windows and the parlor. Merrick stood opposite him, blocking the way to the front door. Both stared at each other in open hatred as Ellis stood between them, her back against the locked door.

"However did you manage it?" Merrick asked. "Escaping from Ellis's little trap room, I mean."

"I had a little help," Jonas said.

"Ah!" Merrick smiled as he nodded. "The soldiers, of course. The one group I couldn't send away."

"Friends are often very useful in a crisis." Jonas shrugged. "But then you would hardly know that."

Ellis felt her chest constricting, her breath coming in painful gulps. "You two . . . *know* each other?"

"Like a newspaper knows a fly," Merrick said. His voice was low and threatening. "Get out of my home, Jonas."

"You have no home," Jonas snarled. "All you have are lies—not even shadows or smoke. Everything here is just wished-for dreams and nightmares. All you do is play at life when there was never any life in you . . . not even an idea of what life really means."

"This *is* life!" Merrick screamed. "This is the life *I* created!"

"And where are they now?" Jonas asked, stepping toward the parlor. "Where is this life that you have created? Show them to me."

"He can't. He k-k-killed them," Ellis stuttered as she spoke to Jonas, her teeth chattering uncontrollably. "Alicia, Ely . . . I don't know how many more. There are bodies stacked up in the carriage house—"

"They're all for you, Ellis," Merrick said, indignation coloring his voice.

Ellis stared at Merrick in horror.

"I have shaped and reshaped my day for you, but it isn't enough!" Merrick seethed, his words forced out between clenched teeth. "I've reshaped the world to suit you, but it's *still* not enough! I killed them all for you and it's still never enough!"

"No, Merrick." Jonas shook his head as he spoke. "You can't kill something that has never lived—but there are other ways to die, aren't there, Merrick? They have no real bodies, but their souls, on the other hand . . . you *could* do something about that, couldn't you, Merrick?"

"I did this all for her," Merrick said as he turned to face Jonas. "Killed them for her! The painter had to die because she had been a painter and would never paint again!"

"That's a lie," Jonas countered. "She would paint again—crippled or not!"

"And the music?" Merrick snarled. "The piano music in her had to die, too! How could she possibly ever play again?"

Jonas shook his head in defiance. "She would find a way. Through work . . . through pain . . . that was who she was!"

"Who I *was*?" Ellis screamed.

Both Merrick and Jonas turned toward Ellis.

Ellis could feel her mind spinning outward, the threads of conscious reason unraveling within her. Her thoughts were like the patchwork quilt of the Disir sisters, only she could feel the stitching that held the patchwork of her sanity coming loose.

"Tell me." Ellis shuffled with staggering steps to the floor between Merrick and Jonas. She spoke quietly, almost pleading. "You think you know so much about me . . . who do you think I am?"

"Your name was, is, Ellis Harkington Kirk." Jonas looked at her, his green eyes brimming over.

"And you say that I *am* dead?" Ellis asked, a strange, singsong quality to her voice.

"Ellis!" Merrick growled under his breath. "Do not listen to this fool again! He's brought you nothing but pain and heartache!"

Ellis ignored Merrick, staring at Jonas with feverish eyes that demanded an answer. "Am I dead?"

"No, not yet." Jonas sighed. "Your body is still struggling to survive in a cold, dark place far away from here—"

"And here . . . where is here?" Ellis demanded, her hands shaking at her sides.

"It is Gamin," Merrick said. "It's your home."

"Home is a place very far from here," Jonas corrected. "This is the 'Tween'—a place far beyond the world you know as home."

"Beyond heaven . . . beyond hell," Ellis said, her voice heavy with sadness. "Captain Walker told me a story of those who were doubly damned: unfit for either heaven or hell. Is that where I am? Is that my home?"

"She came with me, Jonas!" Merrick snarled. "She was never yours, but that didn't stop you from pining for her on the far side of the gate, did it? And when you saw your chance you stole her like a thief from the world she helped build—"

"Home?" Ellis repeated, tears flowing from her wide eyes.

"Call it whatever you will, this is where you belong, Ellis," Merrick continued, a longing in his voice as he spoke. "We made this place, you and I: word by word, line by line, drawing by drawing. We started the day, made up the rules and led all our friends out of the Umbra to a place where we could play. There were those who left now and then—some with Dr. Carmichael and some with the soldiers—but we had fun here, you and I. I was happy then. But then you left, too, and I had to play the game without you. It wasn't fair, Ellis, you leaving me here with Jenny. And then you, out of all those who left, it had to be you that came back—and now this 'outsider' wants to take you away from me again? No, Ellis! It's not fair! This is *my* game and it is not fair!"

Ellis laughed hysterically, a hideous, unhinged cackling.

She turned, staggering as she tried to maintain her balance and her sanity all at once.

"Fair?" Ellis gaped at Merrick. "What does 'fair' have to do with any of this madness? I don't know *either* of you! You tell me you've murdered the only people of whom I have any recollection at all and expect me to just accept those deaths as a token of our former friendship? And *this* man"—she pointed at Jonas—"materializes from a cloud of moths in my bedroom, is familiar with me and takes liberties with my person, tells me that I may or may not be dead and expects me to go with him to some magical gate that will bring me back to life?"

A strange-sounding giggle burst from her lips. "I have had my sanity questioned every day since I arrived in this nightmare. *I'm* the crazy one! *I'm* the lunatic! And now I've come to see that I *am* the only sane one here. It isn't *me* at all! *You're* the ones asking me to choose between a monster and a murderer! It's *both* of *you* are mad!"

"Ellis, please," Jonas pleaded, stepping toward her. "We need to find Jenny—both of you need to come with me."

"Back to this gate, I suppose," Ellis said skeptically. "Back to the place where you say I may or may not be dead?"

"Yes." Jonas nodded. "Before it is too late. I can show you the way. Trust me."

"No!" Ellis roared her abhorrence.

Merrick smiled.

The pain in Jonas's eyes was deep. "But, Ellis . . . I've told you the truth!"

"No!" Within the depths of her soul stirred a fire that was

familiar to her. The anger and indignation that had been building in her found a voice. "*Your* truth! *Merrick's* truth! What about *my* truth! *My* truth is that I don't know who I am, what has happened to me, how I got here or where I have to go to get back to myself. You've kept me in this nightmare with no knowledge of my past and no hope for a future. But I—the *real* me—am out there somewhere and I'm going to know who I am!"

Ellis rushed past Merrick into the entryway. Jonas moved to follow her, but Merrick stopped him with a hand to the soldier's chest. "You think you've won, Jonas, but you haven't. You stole her before and you think you can steal her again, but it won't work a second time. I've been waiting for this . . . waiting for you. You should have left when you still could."

Jonas pushed Merrick's arm aside. "I'm coming with you, Ellis. When you find the gate, we'll both be free."

"Free?" Merrick laughed in derision as he turned. "You think it would be that easy?"

"Leave me alone!" Ellis screeched as he turned at the door. "Both of you standing there beating your chests and arguing over who owns me! As though I were your boots or your furniture or your favorite dog! As though either of you *ever* had a right to me. I want nothing more to do with this madness or with either one of you! I'm leaving and you cannot stop me."

"You're partly right, Ellis; I never could stop you." Merrick chuckled. He reached toward the table behind him, picking up a thick rectangular object. "But this is *my* day, Ellis. *I* make the rules. I've been very busy since I left you in your room at Summersend. Very busy indeed."

Merrick held up the object in front of him. The edges of its cover were crisp and the binding barely broken.

"You're threatening me with a scrapbook?" Ellis laughed in disbelief. She turned to the front door.

"No," Merrick replied as he opened the book. "I'm threatening you with what's inside."

Ellis gripped the handle, released the catch and pulled it open.

She froze.

What had been the front door of the Norembega still opened onto the vestibule, but the outer doors were missing. Beyond where had once been the wide circular drive, lawn, hedge and towering trees now lay a long hallway with elegant raised-panel wainscoting below the chair rail and bottle green wallpaper above to the coffered ceiling twenty feet overhead. Four sets of closed doors were set into the side walls with a set of open double doors at the end. A pair of grand staircases swept upward at the end of the hall to a mezzanine on a floor above. Between the stairs, a pair of wide double doors lay open. Beyond them was a ballroom, brilliantly lit, and beyond that more rooms stretching as far as Ellis could see.

"You're never leaving my home again, Ellis." Merrick grinned viciously. "No one is *ever* leaving my home again."

Ellis turned back to face Merrick. "It never ends? . . . You made it so that it goes on forever. . . ."

"Welcome home, Ellis." Merrick smiled in triumph. "Our new home."

Ellis drew herself up. Her head tilted to one side and a

smile of her own slowly brightened her countenance as a memory floated up from the madness.

"Alicia! Come on; I think I can see something on the other side!"

"No! You know it is against the Rules of the Day!" Alicia said. *"He'll be angrier with you than he is already! Let's go back!"*

"But we found the gate! Doesn't that mean we win? We could have our very own day!"

"You can do many things in your day," Ellis said as she turned to Merrick, her hand still bloodstained from the key, and she pointed at him. "But there is one rule not even you can break . . . the gate."

Merrick's smile fell.

"I've been to the gate before with Alicia," Ellis stated flatly.

"Yes, and Alicia came back from the gate with poor broken Jenny, but not you," whispered Merrick hoarsely.

Ellis continued speaking, cutting across his words. "The gate can be moved, yes, and hidden, certainly, but you can never, ever destroy it," Ellis said, holding her chin high. "I found the gate once before and I'll find it again!"

"This is still my game," Merrick raged, "and I've changed the rules!"

"Change the rules to your game all you like," Ellis said. "I just don't want to play anymore!"

Ellis swept through the door, slamming it behind her.

THE END OF PART I